WHAT WE DID FOR LOVE

All her life, independent and vivacious Francesca had wanted to write for *Charisma* magazine. Now her dream had come true, and her first big assignment was to fly to New York to interview the elusive magnate Bradly Wyatt, her boss. Francesca never imagined that she would fall in love, or that Martin would fill her week with a love and passion she had never known before. Then she discovered Martin's secret and her world fell apart.

JOAN WARD

WHAT WE DID FOR LOVE

Complete and Unabridged

LINFORD
Leicester

First published in Great Britain in 1992 by
Robert Hale Limited
London

First Linford Edition
published 1999
by arrangement with
Robert Hale Limited
London

British Library CIP Data

Ward, Joan
    What we did for love.—Large print ed.—
    Linford romance library
    1. Large type books
    2. Love stories
    I. Title
    823.9'14 [F]

    ISBN 0–7089–5584–3

Published by
F. A. Thorpe (Publishing) Ltd.
Anstey, Leicestershire

Set by Words & Graphics Ltd.
Anstey, Leicestershire
Printed and bound in Great Britain by
T. J. International Ltd., Padstow, Cornwall

This book is printed on acid-free paper

1

Francesca smoothed her suit and glanced at her hair as she passed the dazzling marble and glass office block in Covent Garden. The carpet of the plush interior deadened her footsteps as she just made the lift. Her mouth felt dry. She desperately wanted this job. The advertising agency had used her for two years, and although she had enjoyed every minute of it, she knew in her heart that to further her career she would have to move on.

The experience had been invaluable. Fran had written copy for ads in a small way at first, then had done some quite elaborate pieces about their needs. All this had been appreciated but it still didn't eliminate the dissatisfaction deep within her. She had always tried to extricate herself from the secretary mould that had sometimes been foisted on her.

Nervously she stepped out and stood alone in the corridor, wondering how on earth she had the gall to apply for the job. Editorial Assistant to the Features Editor. What a cheek. She'd go through that door and probably come face to face with the *crème de la crème* of London: girls who had probably made it to the top and were one step away from the Editorship themselves.

Fran took a deep breath and walked towards the door marked 'Reception'. The room was empty. Just at that moment a door opened and a man in his mid-thirties stood looking at her.

He held out his hand.

'Peter Barnes, Editor in Chief.'

His face was kind, and she liked him immediately. Francesca held out her hand and received a warm handshake, then he ushered her into his office. She felt at home immediately. The room was crammed with cuttings from newspapers and magazines. A graphic designer's board and layouts for a job lay under a lamp near the window. She smiled and relaxed for the first time since entering the building.

'Tell me about your present work?' he asked, sitting behind his desk.

She told him how she had studied as a graphic designer, had become interested in writing, but had never been allowed to take on her own clients. He sat, shoulders hunched, looking over the portfolio she had brought with her and listened intently as she explained why she had done certain things; what had motivated her. He leaned back in his chair and described the job she would be taking on if he employed her. When he had stopped talking, he was standing up against the window staring down at the piazza below.

'Well, you won't have a minute to breathe.'

'You mean . . . if you offered me the job, could I do it?'

'Yes, something like that.' His eyes twinkled.

'Yes,' she said firmly. 'I'd find it no trouble at all to fit in with your team and reach deadlines.'

'Welcome aboard,' he chuckled. 'When would you like to start?'

Fran had stood up to shake his hand, but slumped back down into her chair again when the full impact of what he had said hit her. She was going to write for a living. 'I have to give notice,' she smiled ruefully, 'that's only fair. But I should imagine two weeks' — she glanced at the calendar on the wall — 'say the fourteenth,' she finished brightly.

'I look forward to seeing you on the fourteenth. Incidentally, Grace Black, for whom you'll be working, completely trusts me to decide who her new assistant shall be.'

Fran had thought it strange that her immediate boss had not been in on the interview, and was glad that Peter Barnes had mentioned it.

'She'll be back Monday, so if you give her a ring perhaps, and have a chat with her. Introduce yourself.'

Fran nodded. 'I'd like that.'

'Good, that's settled then!' Peter Barnes looked pleased. Grace had been under tremendous pressure: firstly without an assistant, then her health not being up to par. 'You should make a world of difference to her.'

No more pleasantries were forthcoming and Fran got the impression anyway that Peter Barnes wasn't the sort who would make small talk for the sake of it.

The ground didn't touch her feet as she practically ran back to her office. It was unbelievable that this job had worked out right. She began to plan what she would do when she arrived on the Monday. At least, mentally she was planning, but physically her stomach did a loop-the-loop when she thought of that first day on the high-powered magazine *Charisma*.

With a sharp click she heard the door

shut and, without turning round, knew that Gavin had entered the room.

'Fancy dinner tonight chick? I haven't seen you for a week.'

'Why not? I've got some news. What time?' Without looking up she repositioned the lettering of an ad that he had asked her to do, and waited for his answer.

'Eight, usual place, I'll leave you to it, can see you're busy.'

For a moment he hovered over the silky auburn hair, then quickly left her to her work.

At break-neck speed, Fran finished the artwork. Covering it with greaseproof paper, she breathed a sigh of utter relief. She was getting thoroughly bored with graphic design and she knew she had done the right thing by making the break. The important job she held in her hand had met the deadline, so with a strong sense of achievement, she locked her office and hurried out into Commercial Road, Hackney.

In ten minutes she was home and

lounging in her small patio garden, sipping iced mineral water on a luxurious lounger. It was warm for April and not a breath of wind disturbed the peace as she pondered on the approaching evening with Gavin.

A crease appeared in her flawless features as a picture of him came into her mind: always considerate to her in spite of the rebuffs she had meted out to him in the past. Perhaps that was his trouble, she mused, taking a gulp of the sharp liquid and causing her eyes to water. Gavin was too kind, too good to be true. If he'd snap at her sometimes when he was in a bad mood, it would give her a sense of relief. Consequently, Fran's feelings for him never rose to the heady heights, established in her mind, that would epitomize her response to the man she would fall in love with. With a little sigh and shiver, she watched the last rays of the sun drop out of sight behind the wide sprays of peaches that she had trained along the wall.

Later, Gavin carelessly lifted her limp hand from the forest-green cloth. They had eaten a simple but sumptuous meal of lasagne, which Mario, the Italian restaurant owner, had made with layers of spinach instead of the usual pasta. They had washed it down with a rich red Lambrusco from his home town.

Now he stood admiringly looking from one to the other as he drank a glass of the red liquid they had offered him. 'Did the lasagne meet with the lovely Francesca's approval?'

'You'd be very surprised if I said it didn't,' she laughed.

Bashfully he drained his glass and busied himself personally tidying their table. Then without another word he scurried away, returning with a large slice of Dolcelatte cheese and another bottle of wine. 'My compliments on getting your new job,' he beamed.

She took advantage of the *bonhomie* to slide her hand away from Gavin's. She felt absolutely nothing for him in a sexual way. The chemistry just was not there. If he noticed that she had pulled her hand away it was not transmitted to his face, and cheerfully he prompted her to tell him about the job.

Fran dropped her eyes to the green cloth. 'It's simple really: I applied for a job which I didn't think I stood a chance of getting in a million years, and I just clicked. Within minutes, Gavin, there I was, Assistant Features Editor, with a thousand pounds more a year. Don't you think it's incredible?' she bubbled.

'Marvellous. Just absolutely wonderful. I'll miss you Fran.'

'I know,' she answered, searching his face. 'A friend of mine also wants a change from her job, and is very interested in mine when I leave. Would you care to see her?'

'What's she like?' His normality was returning as quickly as usual.

'She's had just as much experience as me, but there's someone she doesn't particularly get on with in her design studio and he's beginning to grate on her nerves, that's all. She's twenty-three incidentally, and nuts about swimming and aqua sports.'

At this piece of information Gavin's face not only looked surprised but he became animated as he probed her for more information about his possible workmate. Fran warmed to her conversation again as she saw how interested Gavin had become.

Poor Gavin, she thought to herself. He was such an oddball in many ways. Rarely did women find him attractive, but it gave Fran a warm glow to think that Marge, her friend, might fulfil a need in Gavin that quite obviously she could not.

Later on, in her garden, as she bent to pull a few stray weeds, she told herself firmly that even if Gavin hadn't found a soulmate, she was positively not going to encourage any more lame ducks! She had her own life to lead, and Gavin would have to fend for himself.

The writing she attempted on the

typewriter that evening was produced with much pain. Fran was aware that no journalist worth her salt rattled off a feature from the top of her head, so she set about organizing the clippings she had collected and made notes as to the gaps where more research was needed.

Two hours and at least four articles later, she had good skeleton outlines and most of the research done. Two or three visits to a good library would fill in those gaps and she would be ready to present them to the Editor in Chief if for any reason 'Grace's' column could not be written.

Heart in her mouth, two weeks later, Fran was once again ankle-deep in plush carpets as she found her way to the fourth floor.

Grace Black greeted her with a warmth that immediately conveyed friendship to Fran. She was a big woman, with a plumpness that suited her. She held out her hand and shook Fran's vigorously. 'At last, a helpmate!

I am glad to see you,' she cried emphatically. She picked up a wad of papers and gave them to Fran. 'You're over here, by the way.'

Grace pointed to a large desk near the window. The area was surrounded by potted palms and climbing plants which warmed Fran at once to her new environment. Where she worked had always been important to her somehow. It lifted her spirits, and certainly made her look forward to the day. She dropped the papers Grace had given her on to the desk, then questioned Grace as to what she wanted her to do.

'Your first job is to sort out which of those articles you think should appear in the August issue. Here's the loose schedule of other articles that will go in too, but we need a few fillers. Basically, the magazine will deal with women returning to work. Think you can handle it?'

Fran nodded hard. She'd made up her mind that the only way to tackle this job was to jump in with both feet. 'Just give me the work Grace,' she said with determination.

'That's my girl.' Grace smiled from ear to ear. With glorious relief, she grabbed the phone on her own desk and left Fran to sort herself out.

Meticulously, Fran picked through the sheaf of papers, discarding those that she thought would not fit in with the theme. An hour and a half later she had three piles on her desk: one with suitable themes, one unsuitable. The third consisted of articles that she was unsure about. She looked across at Grace, who was writing. She coughed to attract her attention.

Grace looked up. 'Honey, don't do that. If you need to speak to me, you need to speak. I'm always up to my eyes in it, so you'll just have to get used to barging in on me.' She was direct and to the point, but it was said with much kindness; only a fool would have taken offence. She stood up and walked towards the neat piles on Fran's desk.

Idly fingering the first piles, Fran broke in. 'Those are the suitable articles.'

'OK. You've earned your lunch. I'll hold the fort here, and when you come back, I'll go. Go to the Grapes. Very generous with the ham-on-the-bone sandwiches. None of that vacuum-pack stuff. Try stilton ploughmans.' Grace stopped. 'I sound like an ad on the telly. Just trying to be helpful!'

Fran smiled. She really liked this woman. She spoke her mind, and probably raised hell if things went wrong, but wasn't the sort to talk behind your back. 'See you in an hour,' she called across to Grace.

'Sharp,' Grace said without looking up.

Sharp, Fran noted mentally as she shut the door. What her late return would cause, Fran didn't like to contemplate. She smirked to herself. Grace doesn't know me yet, so she's not to know that I've never been late in my entire life. Well, only once, she admitted to herself, but that was through no fault of mine.

The lunch was everything that Grace had indicated: not particularly interesting surroundings — more worn than comfortable — but the proprietress was friendly and efficient.

Fran relaxed completely for the first time since she had opened her eyes that morning. Her excitement was due, to a large extent, to her slight energy loss. Flicking through a back issue of *Charisma*, she noted the high quality of the writing. If only she could achieve a quarter of that calibre, she would be pleased. She glanced at her watch. Fifteen minutes to go. Draining her glass she placed it on the counter, complimenting the proprietress on the sandwich.

Grace acknowledged her return, and handed her some more papers. 'Take a pencil, and scour for grammatical errors and spelling. Make a note in the margin. Don't on any account attempt to do all of them. Each one you do should be faultless. I will be overseeing anyway, but it'll save me a lot of the donkey work.'

Fran wasn't surprised at this honest statement. It was something she was beginning to expect. Grace bustled out.

Fran looked round the office. Editorial Assistant. She felt like hugging herself. One step nearer to her goal. She sat daydreaming for a while, and wondered where she would be in five year's time. Sighing, she swept her hand through her hair and pulled the first manuscript towards her, putting all her concentration into the job in hand.

Half an hour went by before the phone rang, startling her, so totally immersed was she in the job she was doing.

'Grace Black, long distance.' The voice was very male, with a richness and depth that conjured up a picture of someone dark and decidedly handsome. The alluring tone intrigued her. 'This is long distance New York.' The voice insisted. Summoning her wits,

16

she answered swiftly but briefly. The call must have been an expensive one. 'Grace Black is out to luncheon. I can take a message, or I can ask her to call you back on her return. Which would you prefer?'

To her surprise the man didn't answer her question immediately. 'Who's that?' the voice demanded. 'It's not someone I know.'

'I shouldn't think so, this is my first day here,' Fran said anxiously.

'What's your name?' the caller insisted, obviously in no hurry to ring off.

'Francesca Spencer, Grace Black's assistant.' There was a slight pause.

'This is Bradly Wyatt.'

Fran gasped audibly, then sucked in her breath. She didn't want to appear like an awestruck teenager. Bradly Wyatt was well known in publishing circles for his flair for buying up failing magazines, and turning them into dynamic glossies. He had just bought up their magazine *Charisma International* in New York as well as the one in London. He also had a notorious reputation with women, and Fran guessed after producing a mental picture of him, that she would have to guard her tongue.

Strangely, she felt the voice didn't match the reputation. She had to admit that although it had an obvious sexual quality, there was also an unexpected note of kindness. This was a man of the world. A man who lived in New York: In the fast lane, she imagined. It took five seconds for these thoughts to rush through her head. Sharply she was brought back to the present by his voice.

'Hello, are you still there?' it politely enquired.

'Yes, I'm still here.' Her voice quavered slightly. She was glad he couldn't see her flushed face.

'I'm phoning about Grace's visit in November; I'm afraid its going to have to be brought forward to September.'

'I've got that down,' Fran answered efficiently.

'I hope so,' Bradly answered casually, 'or I'll have to phone you again. Not that I'd mind. You sound interesting.'

'Save it,' Fran blurted out before she could stop herself, 'I'm out of your league.'

The laugh the other end was hearty and sincere. 'Looks as though Grace has got herself a real woman at last.'

Fran could have bitten her tongue off at her sudden outburst. But she was slightly peeved at his intimate exchange. Within seconds, he had reduced the conversation to a personal level, thus wiping out all the efficiency that she hoped she would bring to the job.

'Is there anything more?' she said in a controlled but trembling voice.

'Nope, that's it for the present, I guess. 'Bye now.'

The charm oozing through the thin wire that separated them by continents clicked, and he was gone. Fran stared down at the mouthpiece, her mind in a turmoil. There was a man who was potentially dangerous, she thought.

The overtones that had stirred her sexually dormant body with just a few words had somewhat unnerved her. Had she been right to shut him off the way that she had? Fran knew that Bradly Wyatt's lifestyle was a thing apart. Rich and glamorous women hung on to his arm whenever he was seen in public. On the polo field he had more than his ample share of success, being an ardent player. Women were bound to fall for such a glowing, successful personality such as his. With a sigh that she had come close, albeit for a brief moment, to a man of such exciting stature, she returned to the job in hand.

Grace returned punctually filling the room with her vibrant personality.

'How's it going?' She glanced across at Fran's desk.

'Slowly,' Fran smiled.

Grace opened the door and shouted for the sub-editor Charlie. Charlie Evans was a stocky forty-year-old. Years of working in publishing had etched small cracks round his eyes and perched over these were horn-rimmed glasses.

'You must be Fran.' He held out a chubby hand, and firmly shook hers.

'Charlie, have you got five to spare me?'

'Grace I'd give you five months if you wanted them,' he beamed.

Fran noticed that Grace ignored the remark and handed him a layout that had been prepared. 'Take a look and see what you think, will you, and here are some manuscripts that are suitable. Just see if we've missed any obvious clangers or libels, will you?'

Grace turned away and started to dial. Fran signalled to her so that Grace replaced the receiver.

'There was a phone-call from New York.' Charlie paused before shutting the door. 'Bradly Wyatt,' Fran continued. 'He wanted to cancel your visit in November and change it to September.'

'Oh, no.' Grace frantically flicked through her diary. 'It's OK. It's OK,' she repeated. 'It's got to be OK.'

Fran relaxed. She wanted the arrangements to go smoothly as she had been part of them. 'What's it about?' she asked inquisitively.

Grace sat down and leaned back thoughtfully. 'I had this brainwave.' She grinned. 'A reporter's impression of New York. I've never been before. Heard a lot. Travelled almost everywhere else, but New York somehow never seemed to come up. I was supposed to go in November, but Bradly has just bought us out, so we do what the boss says.'

'It should be interesting,' Fran enthused, 'especially as you've never been there before. It'll be straight from the horse's mouth.'

'That's the idea. You think it will work?' she asked Fran with genuine uncertainty.

'Definitely. It's easier to travel. Cheap flights. It must be the sort of thing most readers would want to hear about.'

'Look, why don't you come round

22

for dinner tonight? I'd like to fill you in on it anyway. We've got to get into each other's minds so far as work is concerned. Eight o'clock.' Grace scribbled her address on to a piece of paper, and Fran tucked it away in her purse. She was pleased that her first day had been as exciting as she had imagined it would be. She felt she had made a friend, not something she did lightly or casually, and it pleased her greatly.

The afternoon sun dipped lower, until with a start she realised it was five o'clock. 'See you later,' she called across as she left the office.

Grace didn't look up. 'Don't get lost. Angel Islington.' Fran quietly shut the door behind her.

In no time at all, she was home, washed and changed within the hour. Then she spent some time fiddling with her hair and make-up. Fran wanted to look really immaculate. The combination of her mother's looks and her father's height created a stunning picture. Her auburn hair was straight and heavy and her full red lips below her small nose contrived to make her hazel eyes look like two shining green orbs, with almost the same proportions of a bush baby.

Wearing a khaki silk shirt-dress, she clipped a thick red leather belt loosely round it and finished the outfit with a pair of red pumps.

Although pleased with her appearance now, she had no idea of the effect it had on the male population. The natural, easy grace with which she wore her clothes, and the speed with which the whole effect was produced, were matched by her obliviousness to how she stirred the men who passed her in the street. Like an animated woodland creature, she slipped on a white wool jacket and made her way to the Underground station.

Duncan Terrace was a few minutes away from the Angel tube station, and the house was easy to find. As she turned into the square she was reminded of the Sickert painting she had once seen in an art gallery. She stopped and drank in the scene before her, as it was still light.

Tall plane trees flanked the square around which the elegant houses stood in Georgian splendour. She stood outside the black door, pressing the brass bell. A friendly-looking woman opened the door and ushered her inside.

'In here!' Grace's voice echoed through the hall and the Creole woman laughed.

'This way Fran.'

She took Fran's jacket and led the way down the arched hallway and into the large lounge where Grace stood, dramatic in a black silk trouser suit.

'This is home,' she said simply, waving her arm in a sweeping gesture.

'It's lovely,' Fran said sincerely, taking in the scene.

Large splashes of colour decorated the wall in the form of modern paintings. Richly coloured Peruvian rugs thrown casually on to a polished wooden floor gave an air of casual smartness in keeping with what she would have expected of an editor's home. There were books everywhere and a homely, lived-in look. Certainly, the bookcase which reached the ceiling had a worn air about it.

'Sherry?' Grace picked up a bottle.

'I prefer Martini, if you have some.'

'That's what I like. A woman who knows her own mind.' Grace chuckled, looking pleased, and handed her a glass.

'How long have you lived here?' Fran asked, standing to look out at the trees heavily laden with leaves.

'Since I was born. Not here, down the road. I grew up here when Islington was a bit seedy. Well, not exactly.' Her face was lifted up dreamily to the ceiling. 'We were poor. I went to school here. Grew up here, buried my husband here.'

Fran fell silent. She hadn't realized Grace had been married. Somehow she looked as though she had been a career woman all her life with no attachments.

'When he died, I inherited all that his mother had left him, and my career suddenly took off. I could afford this, so I bought it, just before prices soared.'

'You were lucky,' Fran said softly, trying to lift the sadness that had crept into Grace's voice.

'Yes, Jack would have loved this. He always wanted to live in this square. He lived in the flats down in Essex Road. They were named after Sickert, the painter. Sickert Court. Have you ever heard of him?'

'As a matter of fact I have.'

'Jack always had a feeling for the guy. This is where this place comes into it. Sickert lived here.'

'Really?' Fran looked with renewed interest. 'How amazing.'

'Isn't it? I'll never leave here, you know. Not for all the money in the world. It's like a shrine to Jack in a way.' Briskly she got up. 'Follow me, dinner is in the kitchen.'

She stalked off down the arched and corbelled hallway into a cosy breakfast room. In complete contrast to the lounge, a sturdy Welsh farmhouse table dominated the room. Its grained legs were thick and bulbous. The scrubbed top was laid with red linen and place-settings of chunky black china. Grace served a simple chilli-con-carne with red wine, and chunks of brown bread with garlic butter, then simply laid out a cheese board. It was only then that she attempted to discuss the nature of Fran's visit.

Fran had taken the precaution of bringing a notebook, and although her head was fuzzy with the excellent wine, she now summoned all her expertise to concentrate on Grace's planned visit to New York.

'This might turn out to be a bit of a lecture, but should I ever be out of the office, you'll know what's going on. Like for instance when Bradly Wyatt called.'

Grace shifted on to one of the chintz armchairs and indicated for Fran to do the same. 'Now, let's talk about the easiest of the assignments. Not that anything to do with journalism is easy,' she emphasized. 'First Impressions of New York. The idea behind it is that an experienced writer descends on the Big Apple, exploding myths, exposing dangers et cetera, if there are any, telling the readers whether they'd be safe to go it alone. Remember ninety per cent of our readers might be divorcees, single women, older women. We outlive our men. Get the idea?'

Fran looked up. 'Could the single woman afford it?' she interrupted.

'You've got it.' Grace beamed. 'That's the angle, but I want somehow to be specific in the article. Remember this article might dominate the issue. There will be ads from American Express, TWA — you know the sort of thing. It shouldn't be too difficult to get those in. Anyway, what I was saying was that I wanted to guide our reader to places where she can hone in immediately she gets to New York. It must be pretty frightening if you don't know where you're going, so *Charisma* readers must be' — Grace gave a little movement backwards and forwards with her head — 'sort of protected.'

'What about a competition for the reader who writes the best two-hundred words about their favourite holiday venue? What they found to do there . . . ?' Fran asked.

Grace looked positively alive with interest. 'With the winner going to New York for a week,' she finished.

Fran shouted excitedly, 'Can we afford Concorde?'

Grace laughed. 'No, you chump, but Concorde can.'

Fran put down her pen, the adrenalin racing inside her. She could see it now. The lucky reader or readers. She opened her mouth to speak.

'Don't say another word until I've made coffee.'

'Now what were you going to say?' Grace smiled, happily conscious with every passing minute that Peter Barnes had chosen a gem of an assistant.

'Only that you mentioned ninety per cent of our readers are single or on their own. Why should the competition fall into the same pattern as other magazines? Why not a ticket for one?'

Grace looked thoughtful. 'Won't it upset our married readers?' she queried.

'Not if women are seeking their liberation. After all, just think of the test it would be on the marriage, if she won a ticket and he had to decide yea or nay whether to let her go!'

'I wouldn't fancy his chances if he wouldn't let her.' Grace laughed. 'Well, we'll have to work on that one, but we're not in the business of smashing up happy marriages, you know.'

'Good heavens, no,' Fran said vehemently, 'that was the last thing on my mind. I was thinking of the independent woman enjoying a week alone.'

'Righto, we'll put that on the file. But seriously what do you think of the idea?'

'It's great, and original. Especially the cheap places to stay, and what to do with yourself in the evening. It's wonderful and gets right away from the boring generalizations that usually fill up the women's features pages.'

'Good.' Grace nodded. 'Now,' she said, pouring out more hot coffee. 'Now for the difficult bit. Long before Bradly Wyatt took us over, I was negotiating with him to do an interview. He has consistently refused to give them. The only reason he is doing is as a favour to Jack's memory'.

At this announcement, Fran's eyes opened wide. 'They knew each other, years ago, as students. For some reason they hit it off. Jack was older than him: Jack poor, Bradly rich. But Bradly had no family of his own then, and when Jack brought him home during the holidays, he sort of took on the family as his own. He was devastated when Jack died. So there you have it. We've got our world-exclusive interview through my husband's death'.

Fran was silent for a moment after the sadness of the circumstances that had led to Grace's scoop. Then a thought struck her. 'But surely,' she said slowly, 'there must be a deeper reason why Bradly Wyatt won't give interviews.'

'You're a shrewdy,' Grace said, cocking her head to one side. 'Yes there is: his wife.'

2

Grace sat back on the antique chair, obviously toying with the idea of telling her all. Fran didn't hurry her. She had read the occasional article featuring Bradly Wyatt. Each time it had left her with a feeling that although women were in abundance in his life he had no real regard for them.

It had occurred to her that his looks probably prevented him from ever having a sincere relationship with any of them, even though she had never seen him. Models and film stars and the inevitable hangers-on at the polo pitch, all hung round him like bees round a hive, but those same women, she had read in the gossip columns, were nearly always to be seen dancing in the arms of other escorts. Maybe like followed like. They were all of the same ilk.

Grace placed her cup in the saucer. 'Bradly can't help his looks. He attracted, in Jack's opinion, all the wrong women. You see, he became successful very quickly, owing to his father's money. A Canadian publisher, owner of the *Toronto Mercury*, he owned dozens of small magazines. Bradly, his only son, was watched like a hawk, and the old man tried to make sure that only the right women were introduced to him. Unfortunately the old boy was so blinded by what he wanted for his son, he couldn't see the scheming shrews who were ready to pounce on him. Bradly's father held the most magnificent parties in Toronto, where they eventually settled. There was only one aim, to find a suitable wife for Bradly.'

'What did Bradly think about that?' Fran said, looking concerned. 'Surely he had thoughts of his own on the subject.'

'Oh yes,' Grace grimaced, 'he sure did. And I suppose the trouble started from there. He was sent to an English public school which he loathed and detested. Then he moved on to university, Oxford to be precise. It was an all-male college. You get the picture. Up to the age of eighteen only rich little girls at parties in the holidays, then Oxford, where he entertained in true Wyatt style, but still no woman to speak of. Then to college to learn the rudiments of the printing trade. It was there he met Jack.'

'Surely things changed for him then?'

'Oh, very much so,' Grace said seriously. 'Jack used to take him to pubs and they liked football. Then Bradly's parents died suddenly in an air crash. He was left the entire fortune and the responsibility of the empire. But that wasn't the important event. Just about the time they died, a conniving little bitch called Venetia Cullen wormed her way into his affections. God knows how. Jack met her once and loathed her on sight. Bradly didn't know what had hit him. He was besotted. He took her everywhere. Dancing, dining, you know the sort of thing. That was in the May. By Christmas they were married and it was shortly afterwards he discovered the mistake he'd made.

'The rest of the story is rather ugly. Venetia openly took other men back to the magnificent house that he bought. Indiscretion was the polite way of describing her behaviour. Jack tried to console him when he was in London. They always kept in touch, but he changed. The bitterness doesn't show but it's there. Shortly afterwards he stopped all public appearances on television and before the press. The subject of his marriage returned time after time, so one day he decided enough was enough. The press had a field day abusing him. He had been their bread and butter for years. Now he'd shut off the supply of titbits, so they turned on him.' Grace shifted on the chair and said reflectively, 'They always do it. They're like a bunch of hyenas.

Picking the bones until there's nothing left.'

'What was left?' Fran frowned.

'His pride. He'd salvaged what dignity he'd left, and kept a low profile as much as he could. He moved to New York, but it took years for him to emerge into society again. Eventually, of course, he was seen in fashionable magazines, dancing with glamorous women, escorting them to the theatre. According to the stories that circulate, he's hard and ruthless. He uses women like pencils, throws them away when he's had enough of them. So you can see we're damned lucky to get this interview. Thank heavens he knew Jack. We could do with an exclusive like this to lift sales.'

'You're looking forward to the trip aren't you?' Fran speculated.

'It'll be one of the best pieces of work I'll have done,' Grace said in a low voice. 'I have a feeling for the guy. He's not just a celebrity. He's been given a set of cards that are full of jokers; he deserves an ace somewhere.'

'Or a queen,' Fran interjected.

'Or a queen,' Grace repeated. 'Say, have I touched you with the story too?'

'I feel as you do. He's had a rough deal, and from what you've said, he certainly deserves something better.'

Grace was quiet for a while. 'The article won't be as probing as our readers will probably want. According to general theory, we journalists are supposed to stop at nothing to get our story. When I do a story I'm always reminded of T. S. Eliot's line 'pinned and wriggling on a wall'. When I'm sitting in front of my celebrity he or she is at my mercy. I can say exactly what I like. I can be as heartless as the rest, but Bradly Wyatt, I somehow feel personally responsible for, even though he's my boss. Do you understand Fran?'

'Yes I do.' Fran nodded hard. 'I'm wondering though what you are going to say in the feature that hasn't been said before, if you're going to protect him.'

'I'm not protecting him, but I am going to go lightly,' Grace quickly rejoined. 'It could be approached from a sports angle. He's won numerous cups for polo. I saw him once at Windsor. You can't imagine the sight he made on his black horse. He had a white shirt on and cream jodpurs. There wasn't a woman there who wasn't watching his every move. He only had to move and they cheered.'

'I feel a bit guilty about what I said to him this afternoon.'

'Why, what happened for Christ's sake? You didn't upset him?'

'No, but he made a comment, that's all.' Fran looked down at the brandy she had been given.

'What sort of comment?'

'Nothing much, just that he said he wouldn't mind phoning me again as I sounded interesting.'

'So what did you say that made you think you might have upset him?'

'I said I was out of his league.'

'Oh my God, was he annoyed?'

'No, as a matter of fact, he laughed rather loudly. Said something about Grace having found a real woman at last.'

'Well it doesn't sound as though much harm has been done.'

She smiled across the room. 'If he phones again when I'm out, I want you to find out exactly how much time I will have for the interview and where. The day is important. I want to arrange the flight so that I see him the following morning.'

Fran snapped her notebook shut and stretched. 'I've had a lovely evening. Lovely day in fact. When you're interested in your work, it isn't an effort.'

'You don't know what it means to me to hear you say that. There are so many in our business who while away the time in pubs, thinking that they are picking up gossip which will turn into a feature.'

'And doesn't it?' Fran lifted an eyebrow. 'I was under the impression that's how it happens too.'

'Not at all,' Grace said in a heavy voice. 'By all means go and have a lunch time drink. One drink, then change to mineral water. While your lead gets more forthcoming with his information, you stay sober.'

Fran laughed, but she could see that Grace had strong feelings about the subject.

'To do articles as we have to, takes a lot of hard research. It won't be bopped off on an Olympia typewriter in five minutes after a pub crawl. Learn how to take your leave when you've picked his brains and got what you want. Don't get me wrong. Mixing in the right circles can give you an exclusive. I'm thinking of nightclubs. Smart discos. You might get friendly with the manager, who can tip you who's there.'

Fran listened hard. This kind of information was extremely valuable to her. The cheerful housekeeper arrived with her coat. Fran slipped it on and picked up her notebook. She would translate her notes tomorrow during her lunch-hour, in the office, just in case Bradly Wyatt called.

When she arrived home, she poured herself an orange juice and stood thoughtfully on the darkened patio absorbing the fragrance of the night-scented stock. A moth flitted round the tiny light that nestled amongst the flowers, but her thoughts were a thousand miles away in Manhattan. She pictured a lonely man pretending to enjoy himself superficially, when deep inside his heart was torn apart by his fate.

To have the love of a partner, someone who would share laughter with you, eat with you, wake up beside you, must be one of the most wonderful experiences of life. He had been denied that love throughout his life and it had turned him into a ruthless conqueror who took what was flaunted without thought, almost making up for the barren years of male-only confines.

She surmised that he probably ate alone most nights, then did what was expected of him over the weekend: a fashionable restaurant, a beautiful girl, a casino or two, the drive home and coffee. Fran swept her fingers to the back of her neck. What next? Would he bed a different woman each weekend? Her thoughts dwelt on his face and the sensuous voice she had heard that afternoon, and she had no doubt in her mind that he would make a perfect lover.

She felt a slight stir within her as she wondered about him. The tremulous feeling was still there when at last she closed her eyes. Time in London, 12.30: New York, 5.30.

★ ★ ★

It wasn't until the leaves fell on to the patio one morning that she realized with a jolt that August was nearly out.

The 'Red Hot Pokers' and poppies splashed brilliant colour in her fading shrub garden.

With a rush, she realized her diary was never empty and she was having difficulty in fitting in her home life. She finished her coffee and ran upstairs to put on some make-up. Within minutes she was on her way through Covent Garden to her office.

She had been doing her job for five months now. How the time had flown! She'd made so many friends, and although life had been frantic, she wouldn't have altered a single day.

'Hi,' she called to Grace, who was disappearing into their shared office. 'What's new?'

'Don't,' Grace groaned. 'I had to twist their arms at TWA to get me the exact flight. With only ten days to go I could do without hassle.'

'Did you get what you wanted in the end though?' Fran said, shutting the draught that was coming into the room by closing the window, and proceeding to spray the plants.

'Of course, don't I always get what I want?'

Fran smiled knowingly. In five months, she had got to know Grace pretty well. There had been many impromptu meals, a few parties and suppers at Grace's house and her own. Fran realized how lucky she was to have met someone like Grace to teach her the job.

Fran got out her diary and flicked through until she reached September. Grace was writing the dates down and Fran wrote in red in her own diary as Grace spoke. 'Got a number I can ring if I need you?'

'Yes.' Grace shuffled the papers around and found the number of the Pickwick Arms, and the *Charisma International* offices. 'They've given me an office there, which is good of them. Typewriter, secretary if I need one, the lot.'

'That's wonderful Grace, at least your evenings will be free.'

'Huh, wanna bet?' Grace smiled. 'I'll be lucky if I leave the office before nine in the evening, grab a sandwich and crash out till the morning.'

Wistfully Fran thought about the exciting time that was ahead for her colleague. Perhaps next year they could do an article on the Bahamas — first impressions. But she stayed silent and opened a file on her desk. Grace might think her frivolous if she broached the subject just when her mind was on sorting out the details of her impending visit to New York. Anyway, that was always assuming Grace thought her good enough to get into print. She had a long way to go.

There was another call from New York when Grace was out.

'Its Mr, Mr Wyatt,' Charlie stuttered.

Swiftly Fran signalled to him to stay calm, and asked her caller if she could ring back in five minutes. That done, she grabbed the phone, much to Charlie's relief.

'Fran Spencer here, Grace Black's

assistant. Can I help you?' To her annoyance, when she put off a valued contributor to the magazine, Bradly Wyatt was chuckling. She literally counted to ten and took a deep breath before speaking. This man was insufferable at times.

The caller cleared his throat. 'Miss Spencer, have you your notebook?'

She stared at the mouthpiece and whispered to Charlie that everything was OK. He almost ran out of the room, but she couldn't for the life of her see why he was so frightened of Bradly Wyatt. He was only flesh and blood.

She detected a note of mockery in the voice from New York. 'I've always got my notebook, Mr Wyatt,' she challenged. 'You should know that'.

There was a slight pause. 'Right, firstly I won't be meeting Grace as promised at JFK, so she'll have to take a taxi. Got that?'

'Every word,' Fran repeated in an equally mocking voice.

'What's the weather like in London?'

The sudden change of subject was so abrupt she frowned. 'Er, well . . . it's — ' Stumbling over her words, she was interrupted.

'Come along Miss Efficiency, don't keep your boss waiting.'

Fran came to her senses sharply. Ignorant pig. Right — if he wants the weather forecast, he can have it. 'There's a light blue sky, with puffs of cloud. The breeze is light to moderate. Sort of strong enough to bend poppies, but not strong enough to blow your hat off.'

There was a deadly silence at the other end of the phone and she wondered if she'd gone too far this time. Remembering what Grace had said about upsetting him, and not getting the interview, she decided to say no more.

'Well, Miss Spencer, centigrade?'

'Fifteen, so its warm for England,' she mumbled.

'And did you wear a hat today Miss

Spencer?' The voice had taken on that sensual tone again.

'I don't wear a hat, my hair's too springy and thick,' she blurted out.

'And what colour hair have you got? I'll bet its black,' he said seductively.

'Its auburn . . . Look, can we stop this conversation? It's getting a bit ridiculous.' She dropped her voice. What on earth would Grace say if she walked back into the room now?

'I'm rather enjoying it. I'm trying to guess what colour eyes you've got.'

'I think you're flirting with me,' she said boldly.

'Perhaps,' he said lightly, 'but then most women don't mind me flirting, whether they're in my employ or not.'

Astounded at the brazenness of his words, she said with deadly calm, 'Mr Wyatt, why demean yourself with a mere employee, especially one who is rather immune to men's charms, and would certainly never entertain her boss. Let's keep this on a business level.'

There was a slight snort the other end, followed by the sarcastic tones of Bradly Wyatt. 'I can see you'll break my heart if I stay on the phone much longer. So I'd better leave. Goodbye Miss Spencer and don't forget . . . No, silly of me, you'd never forget the message.' There was a click, then a purring sound as she held the phone before resting it in its cradle.

'What an insufferable brute,' she said out loud.

In spite of what Grace had told her, he didn't deserve much sympathy if he talked to women like that. She had never responded to men who thought they could just snap their fingers. It was probably a hang-up from her youth. She remembered how her father insisted she come immediately he called, regardless of how deeply she was immersed in a book.

In spite of everything, Fran couldn't help the lurch in her stomach whenever she knew she would be talking to Bradly Wyatt. Whether it was the power he wielded over her as a boss, or the seductive quality in his voice, whenever he spoke, she couldn't quell the choking feeling in her breast. Nor the fact that her breath came in sharp painful pants. By the time she had finished the conversations with him, she felt exhausted.

With only two days to go before Grace departed, Fran was just serving up her dinner, when the phone rang. A quietly efficient voice asked for a Miss Spencer. She groaned; who could that be? She was ravenously hungry.

'That's me, what is it?' Fran asked politely.

'This is Paddington Hospital. I have some bad news, there's been an accident.'

'Oh my God, who, tell me who!' Fran shouted, thinking of her parents.

'Its not a relative, Miss Spencer, or we would not be phoning.' Fran breathed a sigh of relief and tried to stay calm.

'It's your work colleague. She asked

me to let you know first.'

'What's happened?' Fran's muscles twitched.

'Broken leg, fractured arm. She fell down some stairs. She asked me to tell you, she'd like to see you at the hospital.'

'Right away.' Fran said, almost hysterically.

'No, not right away,' the nurse went on firmly. 'A consultant will be examining Miss Black. May I suggest in an hour and a half? Just relax, Miss Spencer, she's in good hands. It could have been very much worse.'

'OK. Thanks,' Fran said in a leaden voice.

She sat by the phone for a few minutes, taking in the full impact of what had happened. Grace wouldn't be able to fly to New York. Which meant, she thought heavily, Bradly Wyatt's interview wouldn't appear in the November issue. Nor would the New York Impressions article. Oh God, all those advertisements that have been placed. What a mess!

Placing the plate in the microwave oven, she arranged a salad. She must remain calm, she told herself. She turned the radio off and ate in silence, forcing the food down, all the time trying to work out what would be salvaged from the mess. Perhaps they could arrange for another famous person to fill the yawning gap that would be left if the Wyatt interview didn't take place.

She left shortly afterwards, and still hadn't solved the problem even as she walked through the hospital doors at Paddington. The nurse on the reception desk showed her where Grace's room was.

Quietly, Fran pushed the door open. Grace appeared to be asleep, one leg raised slightly under a cape on the bed and her right arm in a sling. The slight movement in the room caused her to open her eyes.

'Hello honey,' she said in a tired voice.

Fran bent and kissed her forehead. 'Now what have you been up to eh!' she said softly, the tears welling in her eyes as she saw the puffy blue-black bruises that decorated Grace's cheeks.

'I'm sorry, I've loused everything up.'

'Don't talk like that, we'll have to think of something.'

Grace tried to turn her head, but Fran saw a spark of fire in her eyes. 'I already have. Got your notebook?' Grace shut her eyes.

'On my lap, you know me,' Fran said grinning.

'Right. Now I want you to listen. Listen hard. Don't stop me. I'm almost falling asleep with the drugs they've pumped into me. Its important, and I don't wanna repeat myself.' Grace lay back on the pillows.

'Go to TWA first thing in the morning, and tell them I won't be flying . . . you will. Then go to the American Embassy and get a visa change. Explain what happened.' Grace opened her eyes. 'You're not taking it down, damn you.'

Dumbfounded, Fran was staring at her pencil. 'No . . . I Grace, how can I go . . . I . . . '

'I told you to listen girl, and you're going to. Now write. Passport, visa, ticket . . . clear?' she said sharply, some of the old Grace returning.

'Yes.' Fran looked down at her, waiting to ask some questions.

'Save it,' Grace said fiercely. 'I've had three hours, like you have, to solve the problem. What did you come up with?' She frowned slightly at Fran.

Fran told her of her idea for a different personality, but hadn't solved the fact that the ads were all set for the November New York issue. She told her too, that the Impressions of New York article would leave a huge space.

'Right, now think Fran, think hard. We've got falling sales. We've got an arranged exclusive with Bradly Wyatt. We got more ads than we need for that issue which will give us a fortune. Next, it occurred to me that you've never been to New York either. Am I right?' She lifted her eyes heavenwards. 'Please say I'm right.'

'You're right.'

Grace visibly heaved a deep sigh. 'Then there's our problem solved. You take my place. Save the magazine. Do a good piece about New York. Interview Wyatt and I have a load off my mind.'

Fran desperately tried to put forward reasons why she should not go, but one by one they were knocked down by Grace. Closing her eyes, Grace continued. 'One would almost say you're behaving like a coward now that I'm giving you your first chance to get well and truly into print.'

Fran flushed. 'That's not very kind, Grace. You know how I feel about that.' Fran's face subdued itself a little as she looked at Grace's plight.

'Then what's the problem? You know we're in a mess if nobody goes, so why are you holding back?' She waited. She couldn't do anything else.

Fran moved to the shuttered windows and lifted one slat so that she could see the busy street below. Without turning, she said in an even voice, 'Bradly Wyatt.'

'You've never met him, this is your big chance.'

There was no answer and the Venetian blind snapped as Fran let it go, blocking out the view. 'Grace, I haven't told you . . .'

'Told me what?' Grace's voice sounded tired, and the nurse put her head round the door.

'I must ask you to leave now.' She looked at Fran with an antiseptic smile. Fran gathered up her bag, as Grace struggled to reach her arm.

'Told me what?' she said, breathing thickly.

'He tends to get familiar with me on the phone. I'm not sure I can handle it.'

Grace chuckled. 'Is that all? Christ,

woman, he gets familiar with anyone. It means nothing to him, honestly. When you meet him you'll see. He'll flirt outrageously, but he's dead inside. Like ice. Tin man, got no heart. Used to have, but he's beyond repair. You go for him and get that interview. If I didn't think you could do it, I wouldn't let you touch it with a ten-foot pole. D'you hear me? Go home, and sleep. Get everything sorted out tomorrow. Let Charlie answer all calls, then report to me. Visa will take longest so get to the place early. Most important thing to do when you've done all that, is to work out those questions that you're going to ask Bradly.

'Get something new Fran. We are depending on that issue to sell double our usual monthly figures. And don't ever think I don't know what responsibility I'm loading you with. I know what I'm doing. I've watched you working for months. I know you can come up with what we want. Hey . . . and grab the notes on my desk. In the green file. Some places to go when you get there, but add your own ideas Fran, it's important. Your article on your impressions won't be half as fresh if you're dragging round in somebody else's train of thought.' Grace slumped back and closed her eyes, just as the nurse returned again.

'Just coming,' Fran said, walking to Grace and squeezing her unbroken hand.

She stuffed her hands deep into her jacket thinking hard. After what seemed like hours, but was in fact only two minutes, she willed herself to move towards the Underground. Once home, she put on the kettle and reached for her notebook. On one page she listed all the things that Grace had told her to do on the following day.

Pouring the water on a tea bag, she gave it a brisk stir. Turning the page she wrote 'Bradly Wyatt Questions'.

For a minute she racked her brains as to what she could start asking him, but all she could see in her mind's eye, was a good-looking, possibly dark millionaire. Someone who would regard her as a mere amateur in his field. He wouldn't have the slightest inclination to release his innermost thoughts to her, and she had a rough idea that it was not going to be a world-shattering exclusive, so much as a hackneyed repetition of what had gone before.

The pencil lay beside the pad as she drank her tea. The memories of their brief antagonistic conversations flashed through her mind, and with a start she wondered if he would remember, but then she dismissed the idea. He was too busy. He must see dozens of people a day, every day of his life. Why should he remember a trifling conversation with an Assistant Editor in London?

Having convinced herself that he would not remember, another mortifying thought struck her. Supposing she got to New York and he refused to see anyone but Grace, whom he knew? She couldn't begin to imagine the embarrassment she would feel at having to confront Grace after all her efforts, with no story.

Grace hadn't told her to phone him and tell him that she couldn't come herself, and in her present state she wasn't inclined to bother her any more with such a trifling detail. If Grace thought he wouldn't see her, she would have mentioned it. After all, she did know him.

It wasn't just the rain that made Fran feel low, as she fought her way to the American Embassy. From the minute she had opened her eyes and realized that she had not heard the alarm clock, she knew what the day would bring. At break-neck speed, she had showered and dressed and was out of the house. Now the first real pangs of hunger were gnawing into her stomach. Skipping breakfast was not one of her habits. Influenced by her Scottish mother, it had been a bowl of hot porridge for years.

The wait for the visa rankled. Fran

pictured her desk at the office. If only she had some of those features articles now, she could have been reading them. Eventually, with the visa stamp on her passport, she mentally ticked it off in her mind. One less job to do.

Staff at TWA listened carefully, and then politely fetched the manager.

'Is there no way that er . . . Grace Black can go to New York? You see we've put this ticket on to a master computer, and it will be difficult to erase. Security you know,' he explained. The uniformed manager smiled amiably at her.

Fran began to panic inside but kept a calm expression on her face. The ticket had to be changed. She kept her voice low and controlled. 'Have you heard of Bradly Wyatt, the publisher in New York? He owns quite a number of newspapers and magazines in America and in Britain.' She waited for an answer.

A flicker of recognition fluttered over the manager's face as Fran uttered the words 'Bradly Wyatt.' 'Why yes, yes, I have heard of him. But I don't see the connection.'

'He owns the magazine I work for, *Charisma*. My editor was going to New York, to interview him. I have to go in her place. She broke her leg two days ago.' She gave a small pause, and tremulously said, 'it's imperative I go.'

'I can see it is, and you can rest assured it will be changed immediately. I'll give you a letter and you can pick the ticket up at the TWA desk when you get to Heathrow.'

Inaudibly Fran breathed a sigh of relief as she left the offices and made her way back to Covent Garden. Charlie had coped with everything she had flung at him. It had been a very long day, and Fran felt pleased with herself, that everything had been organized to her satisfaction. Now for home, she thought, and that long-awaited sleep, but not before making a phone call to New York, to let them know she was coming in Grace's place.

3

Kicking off her low pumps, Fran hung her wet raincoat on a hanger over the boiler to dry. She tugged the curtains in her bedroom and stripped, walking naked into the bathroom. As she let the shower pound over her face and skin, she felt every muscle in her body relax. Later, as she sat on the edge of the bath, wrapped in a warm towel, she shook her hair, which hung in great chestnut chunks.

With supper out of the way, she felt a soft glow as she sipped her fresh coffee. The notebook, though, sat in front of her. The questions to Bradly Wyatt were foremost in her mind, and a slight frown puckered her brow.

She lay back, her head resting comfortably on the armchair, trying to imagine what her boss in New York looked like. Her stomach gave a tremendous lurch and she flushed as she remembered his voice. Soft, velvety and totally masculine. If he were here now . . . Her eyes flew open at the thought! Oh, this is hopeless, she sighed. Get your mind thinking hard about those questions. Don't let him get to you. This was ridiculous, worrying about someone she had never seen, and would only see for half an hour anyway.

She wrote, Question One.'Can you remember what you felt on your first assignment, or interview?' He'd say it was a long time ago, when his father made him start at the bottom and behave like a journalist. Then, she reflected, he'd probably elaborate on the Liz Taylor, pigeon's egg ring story. Fran reflected how she'd read the article years ago and how the words had jumped off the page. It had been so alive and full of interest. Yes, she felt sure he'd tell her about his biggest coup.

The problem of how to uncover

the innermost feelings of this famous celebrity, without hurting or upsetting him, remained unsolved for her. Deep inside she felt sympathy for him. His wife had seen to it that whenever he appeared in public she could embarrass him, and it must have been months before he ventured out anyway.

She wondered whether he would want to talk about Jack. Public school maybe. Had he liked it? What did being an only child mean to him? What did he do in his spare time when he wasn't running the business or playing polo?

Fran threw the pen down in disgust. There was nothing in her questions that poked under the surface. She imagined he'd skate neatly round all the questions. There was nothing that would make the article sing out, and she knew it, with a sense of foreboding.

The whole interview was going to be a flop. She could feel it. Unless some sort of miracle happened, she would fail. Fleetingly it occurred to her that she'd sell her soul to be in Grace's place right at this minute, so that she didn't have to meet her fate in New York.

The plane touched down at John F. Kennedy airport, dead on time. Customs was speedy and, as she suspected, efficient. Grabbing her case, she hauled it out to where the yellow taxis waited. A massive Negro, standing about six foot six, stood at the head of a small queue. Fran caught his glance and his whole face broke into a huge grin.

'Taxi?' he asked rhetorically.

She nodded in reply, and protectively he indicated the queue of people. When her turn came, he grabbed her heavy case as though it were made of polythene and swung it into the boot of the car.

'Do you mind sharing this one Miss?' The taxi organizer opened his eyes wide. Hesitating, Fran glanced past him at the disconsolate-looking businessman standing slightly apart from the rest. Why me? she thought nervously.

'It'll be all right Miss,' he said handing Fran a card. 'He's on his own and the rest of the queue are in threes and fours.'

Fran looked down at the card. Merrill Lynch, Fifth Avenue — David Lewis, Stockbroker. She looked up. 'OK David Lewis, Stockbroker, we'll share a taxi.'

The organizer looked relieved, as the man got in beside her. Holding out his hand, he shook hers firmly. 'I sure appreciate this. I've got a very important dinner tonight. You're English, I can tell.' He looked appraisingly at her hair and face.

Fran relaxed; he was friendly and nice. 'Yes, I am — half-Scottish. Fran Spencer.' She tugged at the auburn hair. 'If you look hard enough you'll see the freckles.'

'I'm looking,' he said, his gaze softening. 'Where you staying?' he asked as they approached a bridge.

'Pickwick Arms Hotel, East 51st Street.'

'How about lunch sometime?' He

grinned hopefully.

'Well, I don't know.' She hesitated, her English reserve coming to the fore. She didn't know this man. At the same time something inside her was telling her that this was New York. Life was bound to be faster than London, and she couldn't think of any reason why not. 'Where shall we meet?' She smiled.

'Gee that's great. I'll pick you up at one tomorrow. Then, grinning like a Cheshire cat, he melted into the crowded sidewalk on First Avenue.

As the taxi swung away from Queenborough Bridge she sank back, pretending to herself that she travelled this way all the time. Fingering his card, she placed it carefully in her purse.

After the dark overhung girders of the bridge, Fran was unprepared for the dazzling lights of Fifth Avenue, and the Grand Central spire that rose like an Eiffel Tower in amongst the skyscrapers. She wished she were walking so that she could savour the street properly instead of through the taxi window, but the car muffled all sounds and smells until she, at last, reached her modest hotel.

A ripple of excitement went through her as she changed clothes: the thrill of being in a strange city. The heat was oppressive, but she had known all about humidity and had packed accordingly.

Jauntily and with a slight spring in her step, she felt the warm air hit her after the air-conditioning of the hotel room. It felt like one of those balmy summer evenings she had experienced in London: the sort of evening, when, on rare occasions, no coat or jacket was needed until quite late in the evening.

She revelled in the fact that she wasn't covered up and felt herself to be more attractive than usual as she made for the nearest pizza parlour. It was a fantastic feeling, she thought, to know that she wouldn't get lost, as she did in Italy in the maze of streets. Here in New York, all the streets were in straight lines.

What time she went to bed, Fran wasn't sure. She only knew that she fell asleep to the noise of the honking taxis she kept thinking 'This is the city that never sleeps'.

Fran found Head Office easily the next day on Lexington Street. With a thumping heart she stepped lightly along the corridor, her pale green linen suit making a stunning contrast to her heavy auburn hair.

The sophisticated receptionist looked up as she entered. 'You've gotta be Fran Spencer from London.' A tall *svelte* Puerto Rican girl, dressed immaculately in white and black, stood up to greet her.

'Yes, that's right,' Fran said, pleased at the welcome.

'This way,' she said, ushering Fran towards a room down the corridor.

Inside, a beige carpet softened the whole tone of the beautifully decorated office, and Fran gasped as she spied through the window the top of the Empire State building in amongst the skyscrapers.

'This is where Mr Wyatt wants you to work. I'm Cassy Newman, General Assistant round here. If you want anything call me on twenty.' She pointed to the dark brown phone.

'Thank you Cassy.'

Fran looked round, when she had gone, drinking in the sumptuousness of the surroundings. This was the sort of office they'd give to the Managing Director of a large bank, in London. Nervously, she picked up the phone and pressed the buttons.

'In trouble?' Cassy said casually.

Fran laughed, breaking the tension. 'Not exactly, I just wondered when I would meet the boss, Mr Wyatt.'

'Well I'll tell yer,' Cassy drawled, 'he's a bit like the Scarlet Pimpernel, kinda elusive.'

'OK. I get the message.'

On the way out she introduced herself to the security man on the door of the office block. 'Only staying a week?' he frowned after they exchanged names.

'I'm afraid so,' she beamed at him.

'Well have a good day.'

Walking on air, she made her way along the sidewalk, taking in the scene of smartly dressed young women and men, but her eye was suddenly caught by a bookshop. She went in and marvelled at the design. They must have spent a good deal of money on the interior. Browsing was her favourite pastime. Before she knew it, it was 12.30. Time to grab a bite to eat.

Brushing past the Politics and Computer shelves, she suddenly saw Literary Bestsellers marked up on the shelf. Lunch or no lunch, she'd have to have a look. She sauntered along the floor to ceiling-high shelves of books, when suddenly she stopped. A man's voice could be heard coming from the other side of the screen.

'Sidney Sheldon was born in Los Angeles and lives in Chicago.' Fran frowned hard. The man was wrong:

Sheldon, whom she adored, lived in Los Angeles and was born in Chicago. Not being able to resist the temptation to give the correct facts to the man, she popped her head round the screen.

'Excuse me,' she started and then abruptly stopped. A man of such stunning physical beauty stood before her, that she was totally tongue tied. She had never seen anybody close up in the flesh before who looked so utterly masculine. His thick black hair was long and smoothed back Continental style and seemed to be lacquered; there wasn't a hair out of place. He was tall, and his light dove-grey suit seemed to have a sheen on it like silk, or mohair.

'Sorry,' she mumbled and darted back behind the books, trying to make a quick getaway, but the man held her fast. Turning, she lost her breath, as she saw her wrist was well and truly trapped by a sun-tanned hand. His dark eyes penetrated her green ones.

'What did you want to say?' he questioned.

'Nothing . . . ' She flushed bright pink and stumbled over her words, put off by the sheer presence of the man.

'Come on,' he chided, 'you looked as though you were going to chip in with some gem about Sheldon.'

Fran hung her head. 'I was, but I'm . . . '

'What was it?' he asked politely, releasing his grip slightly but keeping his hand on her wrist. 'My colleague and I are always interested in new information.'

'Wasn't exactly new information.' She lifted her head and met his eyes. She felt her knees go weak as he looked at her. 'Sidney Sheldon was born in Chicago, and lives in Los . . . '

'No, I'm afraid you're wrong, little lady,' the man broke in. 'You must be confused with someone else.'

She pulled her hand away sharply and the older man, who had been listening, apologized but said, looking at his watch, that he had to leave.

'I happen to work for a publisher in London, not that that's got anything to do with it. I just happen to know about Sheldon. Its you who are confused, you know,' she said, lowering her voice.

Whether he accepted it or not, he changed the subject. 'You're English aren't you?' The man smiled.

'Hmm.' Fran nodded.

'Holiday?' he asked quietly.

Fran looked around. She'd heard how Americans liked to listen to the English accent. 'Not really, I'm here for a week doing some research.'

'Oh.' The black eyes turned softly brown. 'And do researchers eat?'

'Yes, but I'm just going to take a sandwich back to the office for lunch, so I can't have lunch with you,' she said briskly.

He leaned against the shelves and straightened an already straight tie. 'I wasn't intending to ask you to lunch,' he grinned.

Fran wanted the floor to swallow

her. 'Serves me right.' She started confidently, but somehow the words drained away as she caught his eyes boring into hers.

'I'm teasing you. I haven't time for lunch either, but if you'd care to have dinner? You can research the restaurant.'

Fran looked down at the sisal carpets. Another stranger asking her to dinner. He held up his hands in mock horror. 'I shall be a perfect gentleman,' he proclaimed, as though reading her thoughts.

'Nobody's perfect,' she grinned, at which he threw back his head and laughed genuinely.

'May I suggest I send a taxi to your hotel; nobody walks after dark?'

'Pickwick Arms,' she answered as he took out a leather-bound pad to write it down.

'Ten?' he asked.

'I do have to cram a lot of work in this week, make it nine.'

'Nine it shall be. Never argue with a

lady.' He raised her hand and brushed his lips swiftly across her palm. A sensational tingle shot through her and she felt herself go a little limp.

He stood watching her depart, and once outside she wondered if the last five minutes had been real. Still in a daze back in the office, she gazed dreamily towards the skyscrapers outside, thinking of the man she would see at nine.

This won't do, she blinked, snapping herself out of the mood and reaching for a sheet of paper. If I do a two-thousand word piece, I should finish by three, she thought, then I can go back to Fifth Avenue and see Bloomingdales.

At the hotel later that night her reservations returned about the forthcoming date. Was she in any danger, she wondered? But instantly she dismissed the idea.

The manager gave her a message as he handed her the key. 'Where were you? One o'clock, Dave. 5624013.'

Darting into the lift, she hurried to

her room and dialled Dave's number.

'I know, you were shopping, and you got carried away.'

'Er,' she faltered, 'something like that. I found this marvellous bookshop. Well you know how it is.' Fran hated the idea of lying. 'Shall we say one tomorrow and I'll buy the first beer?' she laughed.

'Wow, I sure like this independent new woman bit, but,' he altered his tone, 'honestly there's no need. Anyone browsing round New York for the first time is bound to get carried away. *Ciao*!'

Fran smiled and replaced the receiver. He really was an affable young man. Then she set about the serious problem of doing her nails.

Deciding not to wait around in her room, she took the lift to the spacious, softly lit foyer. Trying not to watch the door every time someone entered, she still couldn't help a quiver of anticipation. She flicked through a magazine on a low table in front of her, but her mind was on the door. When he did walk through, the magazine slid to the floor as he stood elegantly hovering, looking in her direction.

'I see you're ready,' he drawled quietly, 'and even more delectable than I first thought.'

Fran swept a shaky hand nervously through her hair. She must be mad, she thought, going out with a complete stranger with hardly an introduction. She fought, and succeeded in stifling a blush, inclining her head. He stood aside as she swept through the thick smoked-glass doors.

A white Porsche stood at the kerb, and instinctively she knew it must be his. The air of wealth about him wasn't imagined. The car and his clothes were incidental to her train of thought. What she noticed most was the manner that commanded others to hasten to him when he spoke. She had noticed it at the bookshop. One or two people had stepped aside and smiled as though he was well known.

The commissionnaire outside the Pickwick stepped forward smartly to open the door as Fran made ready to enter the low car in her filmy silk dress. Her stomach insisted on doing a little somersault.

'Do you like sea food?'

'Can't live without it.'

He chuckled as he pulled away smoothly from the kerb. 'Good, this restaurant we're going to is the best sea-food restaurant in New York.'

Fran, still mesmerized by the size of the buildings and the brightness of the lights, peered through the windows at the illuminated shops. She felt a happiness sweep over her that she hadn't known in a long time. The fact that he had thought out where to take her, pleased her.

'What are you thinking?' he asked, breaking the silence between them.

Wistfully she told him that she was completely overawed by what she was seeing.

'It has that effect on many people.

Can you imagine what the immigrants must have felt when they arrived on the Hudson and saw that skyline for the first time?'

'As a matter of fact I haven't seen the skyline yet. I came in on the Queenborough Bridge, I believe that to see the famous skyline, you have to travel on the Brooklyn. Am I right?'

'Sure. Tell you what, why don't we see it now?' He gave her a fetching smile.

Fran's excitement bubbled at the thought of seeing the skyline tonight, all lit up. 'I'm easy.'

He turned off the avenue and sped towards the famous landmark.

'What's your name?' Fran enquired.

'Is it important?' came the surprising reply.

She faltered. It was those kind of answers that made her feel insecure. Almost like telling her to mind her own business. 'No,' she answered truthfully. 'Why, is it a big secret?'

'Not at all, perhaps I don't like the

name my mother gave me.'

'OK. What name did you give yourself?' Fran smiled, showing her small straight teeth.

'Call me Martin. How about you?'

'You can call me . . . Angelina,' she laughed, 'as we're going to travel incognito. This is rather fun. New country, new name, new job.'

'New job? Now that sounds interesting. Research, you said. What kind?'

Fran shifted in her seat so that she was facing him. The sight of his tanned profile produced that lurch in her stomach again. 'Well, its not exactly research. You're probably thinking of laboratories. I work for a magazine and I've got to do a couple of articles on first impressions of New York.'

'That's fortunate, for you,' he chuckled. 'So you were sent out. They must think a lot of you.'

Fran glanced out as they reached Brooklyn Bridge. 'Not exactly,' she said in a matter-of-fact voice.

She could feel the tears pricking

her eyes. This was the famous skyline that was unique to New York. The enormity of the twin towers that housed Comex, was magnificent. They were like a couple of science-fiction slabs of light, against the dark purple curtain of sky which hung like a backcloth. Their very height shot upwards and dwarfed the older skyscrapers built on the rocks in the twenties and thirties. The scene imprinted itself on her mind, and she knew instantly that she would never forget it. Grace would have loved this.

Fran was suddenly aware that Martin was calling her name.

'Angelina.' He had parked the car and was sitting close enough for his masculine scent to assault her senses.

'Sorry. I was lost in thought.'

'I could see that. Let's get out.'

She slid out of the car, and walked towards the rail, staring across the chasm of black water lit by a thousand lights. 'My colleague was supposed to be here,' she said in a low, choking voice. 'She would have loved to see this. Unfortunately she had an accident at the last minute, and, well, to cut a long story short, Martin, I had to take her place.'

'So now you feel guilty?' He bent to lean on the rail beside her.

'Yes, it's so wonderful, and Grace would have enjoyed this so much.'

'And would I be taking Grace out to dinner and not you?'

She sensed him teasing her. He pulled her chin round and lightly kissed the tip of her nose. A spark of sheer joy shot through her, but nevertheless, she drew back slightly. He, on the other hand, seemed oblivious to the effect it had on her. His closeness disturbed her more than she cared to admit, but clinging to the rail gave her a sense of stability which saved her from losing her self-control.

'Time to go, I think.'

'So soon?'

'Fraid so. I booked our table, and lovely though this scene is, you've no idea how scared I am of the head waiter.'

'I don't believe a word of it,' she joked.

'True, cross my heart.' His eyes twinkled with merriment as he looked down at her, then escorted her back to the car. 'We can come again in daylight. You'd be amazed at how that skyline changes in the morning.'

The brisk, bustling atmosphere at street level almost jarred with Fran as the car glided to a halt outside a brightly lit restaurant. She would have liked a quieter, more intimate eating-place to enjoy this man's company.

Martin took her arm and lightly escorted her towards some steps which led to a basement. 'Don't be nervous, but watch the steps.'

She sensed a little hostility as the doorman stared blankly at her, but as he transferred his gaze over her head, she saw that look again. The transformation of attitudes. He stood smartly to one side to let them enter, and mumbled a few words of apology.

'It's OK Luke.'

An elegant head waiter took over from Luke and was obviously delighted to see Martin. He beckoned Fran to follow him, and she found herself sitting on plush red velvet seats in a booth. The small round table was covered with soft pink linen, and decorated with red carnations and candles. It was a little awe-inspiring for Fran, whose eyes sparkled like the flames.

Martin sat adjacent to her and seemed genuinely pleased that she was his date. Leaning towards her, he placed the menu between them. 'You can choose yourself, and take pot luck, or,' he said deliberately, 'you can leave everything in my hands. But I do recommend the home-made sorbet as a finale.'

Smiling, she pushed the menu in his direction. 'You can be very persuasive. I trust you. Order me a beautiful meal,' she added expansively.

Seductively, he engaged her eyes

before looking down at the glossy card. 'I think you're a prawn fanatic, possibly a lobster fiend. Maybe it's your favourite food.' She pursed her lips to stop herself from giggling. 'Am I right?'

'Not a fanatic, but I do love prawns.'

He chose the wine, and when the meal had just begun, a cabaret jazz pianist started to play. Fran thought it was just about the most exciting meal she had ever had. There was an element of risk in going out with a stranger: a very handsome one, she thought, turning it over in her mind as he looked towards the pianist. She felt she had done something completely out of character. But this was New York; she had to go back with at least one story.

The wine had lulled her with a heady warmth. She was in control, but only just. She'd have to be careful, she thought, in her present mood.

'Tell me about this magazine you work for,' he said softly.

'What I've learnt in the last five

months is that the magazine needs a boost in its sales if it's to stay up there in the top twenty, or else!' Fran guillotined her neck, grimacing as she did so.

'As bad as that?' Martin grinned. 'Why do you stay in a failing company?'

'It's not failing,' she said protectively. 'And it would certainly not occur to me to walk out when things get rough. Anyway, its not going to happen.'

'Going to wave a magic wand?'

'Sort of. I'm here to do a piece of writing for *Charisma* in London.'

'Impressions of New York. Yes, you told me. English people love reading about the New Yorkers. It's a big mystery. Is it really a mugger's paradise? They're not sure. I get the feeling that they'd like to believe it is OK in New York.' Pensively he glanced at the stage, where the pianist had just started singing.

'It'll be my first real piece,' she said, waiting for his laughter. The laughter never came.

He looked seriously at her. 'I imagine you're feeling pretty tense about the article.'

'You guessed it. As a matter of fact it will decide my career. Either I make a good job of it, or I'm finished.'

'Oh, hardly,' he smiled wryly. 'Journalists, and I believe that's what you are, often get their facts wrong. Get taken to court for it too, but they survive. You need one big story to put you on the map.' He shrugged. 'Then everybody will recognize your name.'

'That's a long way into the future, unless Bradly Wyatt turns up with something.'

There was a small silence as Martin looked keenly at her.

'Have I said something wrong?' she stammered.

Martin picked up his coffee. 'No, why should you have? But why Bradly Wyatt?'

Fran suddenly drew back. The interview she had to do was an exclusive. The magazine's sales would be boosted only as a result of that interview. The information was confidential. She really shouldn't be telling this comparative stranger. But it was too late. She had mentioned Bradly Wyatt's name.

'Why Bradly Wyatt?' he repeated.

'Before I answer, can I ask you a personal question? What do you do?' Her eyes looked openly into his, and he hesitated before answering.

'Perhaps I'm a journalist for another magazine.'

She clapped her hand on her head in horror. If anyone from the opposition got one whiff of their intentions, they'd do everything in their power to steal sales. The trauma of all the work Grace and she had put in to try to get ads placed with a New York flavour was too much for her. Hanging her head, she knew she had said too much.

A hand reached out and cupped her sad face. 'I'm joking, please believe me. By sheer coincidence, I happen to work for the same magazine as you.

Charisma International.'

The relief and happiness those few words brought to her, settled the slight tension that had developed. 'That's better.'

She smiled at his bidding. 'What *do* you do?'

'Oh, I'm just a hack like you. Nothing special, so you can relax.' He turned to watch the pianist. 'Now tell me all about Bradly Wyatt,' he said casually, picking up his drink.

4

Clasping her hands together, Francesca bent her head so that her heavy auburn hair cascaded down in front of her, obscuring her face.

He didn't make any attempt to hurry her, but when the heavy curtain of hair parted to reveal her eyes, he reached over and fleetingly touched her cheek. 'You are very lovely,' he said with conviction. She waited, not wanting the moment to end. Leaning back slightly, he murmured, 'Go on.'

'Bradly Wyatt is a difficult man,' Fran said authoritatively. 'He won't give interviews.'

'Is he difficult? Difficult to live with or are you saying it's difficult to get an interview with this guy?'

Fran looked at him sharply. 'Both. It was difficult to get an interview. I'm only surmising he's a difficult man, because when somebody as important as he is takes a stand against the media . . . '

'Did he?'

'Oh yes, though it's not his fault. He had to do what he did. I'd have gone mad if it had happened to me.'

Martin leaned towards her, and gently held her hand. 'So tell me what happened to him.'

'You must know, we both work for him.'

'Yeah, yeah, but sometimes rumours get mixed up with facts. I'd like to hear what they're saying over the pond.'

She stroked the hand that was holding hers, tentatively. He shifted in the bunk seat and she was only vaguely aware that an arm was grasping her firmly round her waist. She was being pulled to him. Fran let the inevitable happen, and he touched her lips gently with his, but as they drew apart he moved away to his former position. 'So that I can see those eyes,' he said, as though her mind was transparent.

'Bradly Wyatt's life hasn't been all that wonderful.'

'Huh, he had money, he inherited magazines from his father, what more does he need?'

'Love?' suggested Fran.

'What's love?' Martin shrugged. 'Here today, gone tomorrow.'

'That sounds very bitter.' Fran frowned.

'I shouldn't have interrupted. You were saying?'

'He's also supposed to be very handsome.' Fran continued. 'Looks, money, women. Yes, you could say he's got it all. So something went wrong, and you know what that something is.'

'Do I?' Martin's voice struck a low note.

'Yes, his wife.' Fran pushed her coffee cup away slightly.

The pianist stood up and took his ovation.

'Let's go'. Abruptly Martin wrote out a cheque, and placed it on the plate, then summoned the waiter.

Tersely Martin opened the door of the Porsche and didn't speak until he had stopped the car somewhere in Greenwich Village. Taking her elbow, he led her up the steps of a well-lit house.

'Relax, I'm not in the mood for love,' he laughed. 'This is where I live.'

Spontaneously she laughed too, releasing the tension inside her. 'Good, neither am I,' she replied, knowing that was not howshe felt at all.

With bated breath, she tried to visualise the kind of flat he would have: sumptuous, elegant, and — she gave him a glance — full of antiques.

Inside, however, the word that sprang to mind was 'dismal'. Nothing furniture in a nothing apartment. The only splash of colour seemed to be a brown leather sofa. This dominated the room in these drab surroundings. It stood on a beige carpet which had seen better days.

'Home,' he said simply.

Hiding her disappointment, she offered to make coffee.

'We'll make it together,' he smiled, pointing to a doorway. 'Through there.'

An equally bleak kitchen confronted her, and although spotlessly clean, it did nothing to dispel her gloom. Obviously he spent all his money on cars, she decided. She poured the milk into the jug, and placed it on a tray. At least he had decent coffee.

Her own house, she reflected, was comfortable and mellow. Fran had always told herself that she got more pleasure from sitting on her patioed garden, looking at her terracotta pots and watching the butterflies settle on the buddleia, than wearing this year's fashionable rubbish.

'Are you going to stand in the kitchen?' Martin's soft voice brought her back to the present.

Their eyes met. His were still bright and twinkling in spite of the lateness of the hour.

'Oh, sorry.' She moved into the

lounge and wandered to a bookcase near the window. His collection of books was a complete mixture, from Shakespeare to Henry Miller. 'You read widely!' she exclaimed.

'Yes, it goes with a job.' She pulled a face and apologized.

'Come and sit down.' He carefully avoided sitting next to her on the sofa and sat opposite in a battered old leather armchair.

'That looks pretty old,' she remarked, unable to resist mentioning it.

'Fifty years precisely.' He rubbed the arms. 'With a bit of luck, it will last another fifty, but the edges of the arms are going a bit now.' He flaked up the roughened leather for her to see. 'My father's.'

'Oh, sorry.'

'Don't be. He was a tyrant. Thought he was doing his best for me, so I understand him, but he made my life, and other people's lives, hell. You don't mind if we drop the subject? This chair,' he smacked the arms. 'I just can't bear to throw it out, although that sounds contradictory. Anyway,' he said, 'my children might want it.'

'You have children?' Fran faltered.

A gleam of interest crossed his face as he stared at her. 'Not yet, but I've every intention of having them. At least four. I'd hate to have just one.' Fran felt a warmth pervade her.

'Now just before we left the restaurant, you were telling me about our mutual boss. Something about the media and his wife.' He fixed his eyes on her, and poured her a coffee.

'I'm not all that knowledgeable about him,' Fran apologized, 'but there's no harm in telling you as we both work for him. I've got to interview him and he doesn't like giving interviews.'

'So . . . if Bradly Wyatt doesn't like giving interviews, how do you propose to get in to see him?'

'It's all been arranged.' She smirked happily.

She enjoyed the look of stark amazement on his face. She, an unknown journalist, had managed to get something that even hardened hacks couldn't get. An exclusive with the owner of one of the World's most prestigious magazines.

'So when are you seeing him?' Martin asked.

'Tomorrow at ten.'

'Scared?' he drawled.

'Wouldn't you be?' she countered. He nodded. 'He evidently hates women.'

'Really?' Martin grinned slightly, and snuggled further into the chair.

'Because of his wife.' Nodding sagely, Fran wondered if she was divulging too much. 'Listen, I've got to say this to you. You might think it a bit insulting after the wonderful evening we've had.'

'Go on, I'm intrigued.'

'This conversation we're having is strictly between you and me. I wouldn't want to spread anything else about the poor man. The press have made mincemeat of him over the years.'

'Go on, but I give you my solemn

promise that not one word of this conversation will pass my lips.' Fran breathed a little sigh of relief.

'Why do you call him 'poor man' ? I take it you sympathise in some way?'

'You bet I do,' Fran said emphatically. 'His wife was a liability to him.'

'How do you know all this?' he asked, looking interested.

'Let's say, I do know. He had a friend years ago who knew him well. I'm fortunate enough to know his wife. In fact I work under her.'

'Things are becoming clearer.' Martin altered his slouching position, and held his chin with one hand.

'His wife could have been so helpful to him,' Fran said wistfully. 'Instead, from the minute she married him, it seems she made herself an embarrassment.'

'Did she love him?'

'I don't know. How does anyone know truly if someone loves someone else? We don't know, do we? What I know . . . is that he had a pretty miserable, lonely childhood. So it stands to reason that he was searching for love.'

'And that's wrong?'

'No, no, of course not, but maybe she wasn't. Maybe she wanted security.'

'Probably.'

'But he put love first.'

'Do you put love first?'

Fran looked at him for a full thirty seconds before rising. 'Time to go,' she smiled. 'You're bored.'

'Not at all, I was just beginning to enjoy myself.'

'Perhaps that's why I'm going.'

He made no attempt to stop her, but outside her hotel he turned to her and kissed her. Fran let the kiss go on, not wanting to draw away from him, all propriety lost in a sensual embrace. When he did release her he regarded her with questioning eyes. 'Do you put love first?'

'Half and half. I don't like going out with men who are going nowhere,' she said softly.

'So they have to be somebody.'

'That's not what I'm saying, and it's late.'

'See you tomorrow. I'll take you on the ferry to Staten Island.'

'I've got the interview tomorrow,' she pleaded.

'I'll phone you at twelve. I don't suppose he's going to talk for more than an hour.'

'You're right. Twelve then, and thank you, I've enjoyed today.'

'My pleasure.' He took her hand and swiftly kissed the back of it.

The bed was cool and her room quiet as she lay thinking about Martin. From the first moment she had met him she had been drawn towards him. The kiss had been a culmination of all she had wanted from him the moment they had met. What an amazing coincidence that they should be working for the same magnate.

A nausea spread over her as she thought about the interview the following day. She reached out to check her questions for the umpteenth time, changed her mind, switched off the lamp, and let sleep envelop her.

The next morning, choosing her wardrobe with great care, she dressed. She could only manage coffee before leaving her room.

Cassy greeted her brightly. 'Big impression huh?'

Pleased, Fran made her way to her office, too nervous to sit, and unable to leave. Cassy was going to call her as soon as Bradly Wyatt arrived. According to the staff, his penthouse suite overlooking Manhattan was impenetrable from the office below. Letters were dictated and sent down in a special lift shaft, just big enough to contain box files. When any business was done, it took place in the adjacent conference room, also served by a special entrance. On each floor of the building there was at least one of his papers or magazines.

Fran jumped as the phone rang.

'David Lewis, Merrill Lynch,' Cassy said matter-of-factly.

'Fran.'

'David,' she piped.

'What about dinner this evening?'

Fran puckered her brow. She really wanted to leave the evening free for Martin just in case he suggested going out again. 'Yes, OK. This evening about seven.'

'Meet you at your hotel.'

'Yes, OK.' She felt flat. Really she didn't want to go anywhere with David, but she had no idea what Martin might be doing. He might be working. He might have a steady girl and his night out with her could have been a one-off.

Looking across at the skyscrapers she dismissed the idea. There was something deeply sincere about Martin. He hadn't tried overly to impress. The evening had been an easy mixture of jazz, food and friendly conversation. There was a distinct feeling in her gut that it was far from casual.

David was speaking to her again. 'Are you there?'

'Yes, yes . . . David, do you mind if I leave early?'

'No, of course not. I take it you don't want to eat?'

'I've been invited to a supper party with someone from the magazine. I'd like to be able to go.'

'Fine, we'll go to a wine bar and I'll introduce you to a few friends of mine. How's that?'

'Lovely David, 'bye.'

Half an hour later Cassy rang to say that Bradly Wyatt was on his way to New York State to meet the Mayor.

'Does that mean I've had my interview?' She swept her fingers through her hair in a familiar gesture.

'I'd put a bet on it,' Cassy said confidently.

She felt let down. She had geared herself up only to be let down. Four days left, she thought, glancing at the calendar. Time was flying and she'd have to get moving if she was to do the articles that Grace wanted.

Fran was lost in thought when the

phone rang, and she heard Martin's voice.

'How ya doing?' he chirped.

'Not so bad,' she answered, a thumping in her chest beginning to take hold of her. 'I've just done a lot of hard work on my First Impressions article. I was miles away; you gave me quite a start.'

'Well how d'ya feel about breaking off to do some more research? Remember I said I'd take you to Staten Island.'

'Where are you now?'

'In the wine bar around the corner, Trelawney's.'

'I'll be right down.' Practically running to the cloakroom, her heart thudding, she tried to quell the excitement she felt inside her. She retouched her make-up and dabbed some perfume on to her pulses and temple: just in case, she thought sentimentally, remembering Martin's kiss.

Humming, she took the lift to the ground floor, then round to the wine bar.

'Hi.' He bent and lightly touched her forehead with his lips.

Summoning all her strength of mind, she positively refused to blush. 'Staten Island, here we come!' she laughed.

Mockingly, he said, 'You look dressed to kill.' Then he turned and hailed a cab.

'Don't,' she groaned as she climbed in beside him. 'It was a complete waste of time.'

'The interview? Why, didn't he like you?'

'I didn't see him,' she said fiercely. 'He went to New York State to meet the Mayor.'

'So you couldn't charm him with those lovely eyes.' He laughed. She tried to give him a withering look, but failed, and ended up grinning. He paid the cabman, and helped her out.

'You seem to be laughing at me Martin. Really it's no joke. This guy's so temperamental, what the hell do I do if he has already changed his mind about giving the interview? I'll kill myself rather than go home empty-handed.'

He drew her to him as the ferry pulled away from the dock. 'No you won't. You'll enjoy your stay in New York and we'll have fun.' Gently he brushed her lips.

Sadly she lifted her green eyes. 'I wish I could be as optimistic as you. I'm beginning to get bad vibes. Maybe he never intended to see me. You know how these celebrities behave.'

'Yes, I do,' he said knowingly, lifting her chin gently. 'Spoilt brat, he's probably not in New York State at all. Bet he's with a woman.'

'No!' Fran said, shocked.

Martin laughed. 'Don't be so serious. If you don't get your interview I'll personally see to it that you get someone. A celebrity from this goddam place. Now, let's enjoy the view shall we, that's what you came to write about.'

He propelled her to the front of the ferry, and told her to grip the rail. She jumped as he came in closely behind her and placed his arms squarely beside hers. She turned slightly and he bent forward, his body moulding into hers. Then she felt his cheek on hers. The slight prickle of his rough chin sent a shiver down her spine. Why did a slight stubble on a man's chin have that effect on her? He hugged her to him and kissed her ear.

The sky was overhung, leaden and misty but somehow it didn't seem to matter. She turned to stare at the Statue of Liberty rising out of the East River like some huge lighthouse. Willing herself not to turn back to see the New York skyline, she listened as Martin continually whispered in her ear not to do so. 'I'll tell you when.'

When she did turn, it drew gasp. The vista of the previous night was just as impressive in daylight. Again, she knew she would never forget this scene, as it imprinted itself on her senses. Seeing the real buildings after the postcards and pictures showed there was no comparison. This was wonderful experience. She wiped the tear that had formed in the corner of her eye.

'Hey, I'm the one who's supposed to feel like that. This is my town!' Martin wiped her cheek with his pocket handkerchief. 'Let's walk through the ferry, after I've taken your photograph.'

She posed against the rail, and then he handed the camera to a tourist to take one of them both. Roughly he pulled her to him, and she looked up into his eyes, just as the shutter closed.

Handing the camera back, the tourist remarked, 'I can always tell lovers, when I see 'em.' And he cackled his way back to his wife, who was leaning on the rail.

Martin remained looking down at her, as their eyes lingered on each other. 'Why, I do believe I detect a blush,' he whispered so softly that only the wind and she could have heard.

A voice inside her warned her not

to let him get under her skin. She was leaving on Saturday and then he would be gone from her life forever. This interlude must not be allowed to cloud her vision.

His dark attractiveness, mingled with an animal-like quality which was purely masculine, made her want to reach out and touch him whenever he was near: qualities which no doubt would affect other women in the same way.

His arm on her elbow, he escorted her towards the stern of the ferry. 'You've gone very quiet.'

'Sorry.' She uttered the words unconvincingly.

'We're nearly at the Statue, take some pictures now.'

She did as he wished, then turned the camera on him, unexpectedly. He gave a slight frown at first as though he hated having his picture taken, then she saw him visibly relax and smile straight into the lens.

Fran heard a clunk as the ferry docked, and the men rushed forward with the chains to anchor firmly on the quay. Martin guided her away from the small crowd to look towards Manhattan. The sky had cleared of the mist, and a hazy sun was emerging from behind a cloud.

'Let's wait here. The ferry will be gone in a while with all the tourists, and then we can go inside the statue.

'Wait till you've seen the view from the top!'

Slowly the ferry drifted away and Fran slipped her arm through his. 'Come on then, don't keep me waiting.'

It wasn't until she had climbed the last step that she realized how enormous the building was.

The huge windows which framed the view of the Hudson and East Rivers meeting, formed the crown on the head of the statue. Helicopters buzzed at a discreet distance yet seemed so close.

'It's marvellous at night,' Martin said, as he observed her interest in the great torch. 'We'll go on a helicopter trip if you like tonight. We can catch one down on the East River. How about it?'

'Yes. I'd like to make it later though, because I've promised to meet someone for drinks at seven o'clock.'

She was unprepared for the effect that her words would have. 'As you wish. I wasn't aware that you knew anyone here.'

'I don't. This is an acquaintance. He shared my taxi cab from the airport.'

'And then he picked you up.'

She could feel the challenge in his voice. 'No more than you did. If I remember, we weren't exactly introduced.' She turned away as his eyes blazed like balls of fire. She could see he was angry, but couldn't really understand why he was getting so heated.

He had dug his hands deep into his pockets and was endlessly fingering his loose change, staring across the water, his expression blank and stony.

Packing her camera away, she linked

her arm through his. 'Come on, it's only someone who wants a drink.'

He gave a slight cluck of his tongue.

'I've put him off twice, to go out with you,' she went on, ignoring the slight sound.

'Thank you,' he nodded, a note of sarcasm creeping into his voice.

Fran pulled her arm sharply away. 'Look, let's get something straight. You don't own me. I've only known you three days and . . . '

'Funny, I got the impression that you rather liked my company.'

Her eyes were stinging with tears at the words that he was forcing her to say. 'Does it mean I can't have a drink with a friend?'

'He's a guy. He's taking a beautiful woman out,' he snapped viciously.

At these words, she flushed scarlet. He was being possessive. Well, he had no right to be possessive. She could see anybody she wanted. It had been years since she had asked anyone's permission to do anything, and she didn't intend that situation to reverse itself now.

They stood in comparative silence on the ferry back to Manhattan and she was thankful when at last the boat docked.

Conversation was stilted and they had walked as far as Wall Street before he hailed a cab and put her in it. Fran was deeply hurt, but her pride stopped her from voicing her thoughts.

'Lexington East 44th Street,' he barked at the driver. 'I'll call you later,' he said, turning to her.

For a split second, alarm shot through the whole of her body with the thought that he might not see her again. She couldn't bear the idea of it. Why didn't she stay with him tonight? Cook for him at his flat? Anything rather than this awful chasm that had opened between them. But there was no time to muster any words because the taxi shot forward and the last she saw of him was his lean figure crossing into Wall Street itself.

'He sure didn't look happy,' the taxi-driver remarked.

'He's got a lot on his mind,' Fran replied defensively.

If Cassy detected there was anything wrong she never commented, but Fran welcomed the coffee she made at 5.30.

'You off now?'

'Fraid so, gotta date.' Her elegant form breezed out and, racing against the clock, Fran wrote another five-hundred words before flicking the switch on the word processor. It had been, after all, a satisfying end to a miserable day. She had written at least the equivalent of three full-page articles and there were four days to go. Grace would be pleased.

Later, after showering and donning a cream silk dress, she almost floated down in the hotel lift. Inside though, her heart was leaden. There had been no contact from Martin and the only prospect now, was to have a drink in a wine bar with a complete stranger.

5

Dave Lewis turned out to be quite entertaining and was interested in her assignments.

'I wish you luck kid. He went out of circulation months back. Fell out with the media.' He started to laugh. 'And you reckon you're going to crack him!'

'Look Dave, I've got to go now.'

'Shall I see you back?'

'No, I'll get a cab.' She leaned over and impulsively kissed him on the cheek. 'Thanks for a pleasant drink.'

Breathing deeply, she walked along the sidewalk for a block. She didn't really have to take the cab. Looking up at the neon sign at the kerb, the traffic lights warned her 'Don't Walk.' She stood waiting, her gaze wandering to the large drain holes in the middle of the road. Thick dense steam oozed from them. Fran glanced back up at the lights again just in time to see them change from 'Walk' to 'Don't Walk' again. Hundreds of taxis and cars thundered past so that she stepped back a pace. Too late: she'd have to wait. Eventually a cab slowed long enough for her to catch the driver's eye.

Having directed the taxi to the office headquarters, Fran stood looking towards the main entrance of the block. The security guard inside was reading. As she approached, he looked up.

'The lady from England.' He smiled broadly.

'Look, I know this is irregular, but I need to do some work.'

'Gee, that's OK. Mr Wyatt just arrived. I'm here all night.'

'Oh really?' Fran's heart thumped at the mention of his name.

'Shall I let him know you're in the building?'

Fran paused for a minute. Would he think it an intrusion on his privacy? It was after office hours. Staff, she understood from Cassy, never interrupted him, even though he was in his suite above the offices. Nevertheless, she had come from England just to do the interview, and he had let her down more than once. 'Y-yes . . . yes, tell him the journalist from England is in the building,' Fran said in a defiant voice, and entered the lift to the fourteenth floor.

She stood looking out at the night and could just see the busy street below. How she wished Martin would show up. She pictured him in his apartment, slouched in the battered old leather chair. Sighing, she slipped the disc into the word processor. Her whole concentration was directed towards the flickering screen, so it came as a shock when the phone echoed round the empty office.

'Hello,' the voice said softly.

'Martin!' The blood rushed to her face, and she stifled the urge to get ecstatic because he had phoned, and kept a tight control over her voice.

'Take a cab to the flat, 20, West Fourth Street.' His words hung in the air like the aftermath of a heady perfume. There was nothing to say, but she managed a husky 'yes' as the tears pricked her eyes.

'See you soon.' He replaced the receiver, and with lightning speed, Fran had cleared her desk and was downstairs.

Getting a cab took a little while, and when she did turn into Greenwich Village, it was gone ten o'clock. The light from the hall outlined Martin standing on the steps. Fran faltered a little. Am I getting too involved? she asked herself. He stepped forward as she reached the top step and pulled her to him with a force that made her breathless.

'Don't let's fight,' he whispered softly, his cheek against hers. 'You're the only real friend I've got.'

'I don't believe you,' she said, nestling closer in his arms. He kissed her deeply, and then abruptly took her hand and pulled her inside.

The flat hadn't changed, and in a glance she saw that he had prepared a quiche salad, which was laid out on the small table.

'For me?' She turned, smiling at him.

He struck his head with the flat of his hand. 'Oh gosh no, its for me and the woman upstairs.'

Fran frowned, then laughed, making a dive for him. They landed in a heap on the sofa, her sprawled over him. He was kissing her hand and caressing her back, sending palpitations through her body. He twisted and made himself more comfortable, placing her beside him. His arm still locked her to him and he pushed back the weight of her hair that inevitably fell forward.

'I'm sorry for what I said this morning.'

She nodded. 'I know, perhaps we're getting too intense.'

'Can we get too intense?' His look

told her what his thoughts were. 'I want to make love to you,' he went on. 'No, don't speak, it's not just a spur-of-the-moment idea.' Seeing the disquieting look on her face, he went on. 'Ever since we met . . . '

'Don't.' Fran disentangled herself. She walked into the kitchen. 'Please.' She turned to face him. 'I'll be gone in two days. You've got to understand how futile this would be.'

'Does it have to be that way?' He sat up, leaning nonchalantly on the arm of the sofa. Looking across at him, she knew in her heart that there was nothing she wanted more right now than to stay here in New York with him. She was falling in love with him. But was he falling in love with her? She knew very little about him. Their incidental meeting and subsequent dates had little to do with love, hadn't they? Fran felt confused. Since she had bought the house in the East End, she had been determined to cling to it as a form of refuge from the misery of her broken engagement nearly five years ago. There had been no one serious in her life until now.

The feeling made her uncomfortable. She had no idea how Martin thought of her long-term. New York probably hastened relationships, but she had a life in England, and what then?

He stood up and, bending low, kissed her bare arm. 'Believe me, angel. I'm not a gigolo.'

'It never occurred to me that you were, but what about me? I can't just hop into bed and then shrug it off when I go home to England, can I?' He looked pleased, which annoyed her. She was being deadly serious.

'Have I said something funny?' she snapped.

In answer, he pulled her up with a force that jerked her body to his, in a fierce embrace. He then gently kissed her. 'You have at least admitted you would let me take you to bed.'

She felt two spots of colour burn her cheeks. 'I'm not sixteen you know, but

I try to think of the consequences.'

'You think too much then,' he answered.

'Martin, you know that I mean. What if I don't want to shrug you off, what if I said, OK, I'm moving in?' She gestured to the flat.

'Would you?' He offered thoughtfully.

'Let's eat, shall we, or I'll call the woman upstairs.'

He threw back his head and laughed, reluctantly releasing her. 'We'll eat.' He pulled back a chair, and sat down opposite her, pouring out a glass of red wine and handing it to her.

'You seem to have expensive taste in wine,' she remarked, glad that the mood had lightened.

'Not at all, if you look in the shops, you'll see that we have very few red wines in New York. Red doesn't travel well from the best vineyards in France. So you won't see many clarets or Rhones. Mostly we drink the Californian wines, but,' he said distantly, 'it's not the same. Have you ever been to the South of France?'

'Collieure, on the French-Spanish border.'

'Then you'll know what I'm talking about.'

'Yes,' she said dreamily. 'We sat out on the patios and outside the cafés, and the wines were always at the right temperature, it was so warm out there.'

'You sound as though you're an expert.'

'No,' she lowered her eyes.

He poured some more wine for her. 'Who was the 'we'?' he asked casually.

She paused and looked steadily at him. 'It was important at the time. Not any more.'

The knowing look he gave her told her a great deal. His quiet interior had been masked by a banter which always made her suspicious. She wasn't in the mood for answering questions. With only two days left, each moment was precious.

'Coffee?' he asked when the meal was over.

'Hmm, yes please. One of the things I like about being abroad.' She leaned back and stretched. 'Your tea's lousy,' she laughed. 'But they can't make coffee in England can they?'

'Nope.' He carried in the steaming jug and placed it on the coffee table. 'How's the writing going?' He poured the coffee, not lifting his eyes.

'OK. I've managed to write about all the places we've been to and some others I've done on my own.'

'What about Bradly Wyatt?'

'Well, I'll be honest Martin, I've got nowhere. I've been put off three times now and I'm seriously doubting that he really promised Grace an interview — she's the woman editor I told you about, who arranged it.'

'Would it help if I got Woody Allen to see you?'

Fran gave him a long hard look. 'Martin, I don't think you realize how serious this is. If I go back without the

Bradly interview I might as well kiss goodbye to the job. I've a mortgage to pay.'

'I'm being perfectly straight,' he interrupted. 'Woody Allen plays in a bar over the road every Monday. He happens to be a friend of mine.' He fixed his eyes on her so honestly that she had no alternative but to believe that he was telling the truth.

Later when he had dimmed the lights and she was cradled in his arms, he brushed his lips over her hair. 'I want you so much Fran, but the time isn't right.'

'Why?' she murmured, nuzzling closer. 'Now I need you.'

Fiercely he bent to search for her lips. Eagerly she reached up and held his head, letting her fingers stroke his hair at the nape of his neck.

'Don't do that,' he whispered hoarsely. 'I'm having trouble as it is.'

'Is there someone else?' she asked.

He chuckled, but not unkindly. 'No, my love, there's no one else, but there are a few hurdles before I can show you how much you mean to me.'

Satisfied, she kissed him passionately, all thoughts of Saturday dismissed in a yearning to stay like this for ever.

'Tomorrow I'll phone you and tell you what time Woody will see you.' Obediently she said she would be ready to fly the moment he called, but half of her still doubted what he said. Tomorrow would tell. Reluctantly, he drove her back to the Pickwick. She was deliriously happy, but dismissed from her mind the dismal prospect of the Saturday flight.

'Goodnight my angel, wait for my call.'

★ ★ ★

She fled to her room needing solitude. Supposing he wanted her to stay? She couldn't. There was the house in London and the mortgage. She slid between the sheets. The flat in Greenwich Village was awful compared to her house off the Commercial Road. Yet if she told her friends they'd laugh at her. Anything in Greenwich would have to be wonderful. That was where the rich of Manhattan lived. They'd say she was wrong. But her house was comfortable and warm. It was hers. She didn't have to ask anyone if she wanted to change the wallpaper, or shift the furniture.

She wasn't ready to throw it all away for love. Did she really love him, if she was thinking more about the house? The torment didn't go away even when she closed her eyes. When sleep did come, it held pictures of Woody Allen playing the clarinet, and Martin offering endless cups of coffee.

Fran tried not to think of what day it was when she woke up. Within twenty-four hours she would be packing for the airport. Who knows when I'll return? she thought as she skipped breakfast and made her way to the office.

Grace had asked her to call in on the

Sunday if she was fit enough, and Fran had every intention of showing her just how creative she could be with this important assignment. This was her big chance and she wasn't going to blow it by sitting waiting for the 'call' from Bradly Wyatt. She grinned to herself, it cheered her enormously to think that Woody Allen might oblige her with his presence. Uncovering the typewriter, she started devising questions that she imagined he may not have been asked.

Martin rang as planned and she felt a smile play spontaneously round her mouth as she mentally conjured up a picture of him casually slumped in his battered old leather armchair.

'He's going to be here at eleven. Sharpen your pencils please.'

'Really?' Fran cried ecstatically.

'I promised, didn't I?'

'But . . . Oh Martin, help . . . what do I ask him . . . ?'

'Now, stay calm. What about his university days? He was thrown out of New York University and the City

College. And don't worry angel. He just talks, you listen. Bring a recorder. Hey, and don't forget he's my pal too. Relax and have fun.'

It was reassuring to just hear the words and already Fran felt less nervous. 'OK, but it's important Martin, that's all.'

'Don't I know? You get down here soon, I need to hold you before he arrives.'

'I'm on my way,' she whispered, the final tension dispersing at the mere sound of his voice.

Cabs were difficult to get, and when she did arrive at the flat the celebrity was already drinking coffee. He was smaller than she imagined, even though she knew he was short. His indolent face immediately brought a smile to hers. He was wearing corderoy trousers and check shirt and the inevitable glasses.

'Hi angel,' he said in a familiar voice.

Fran felt herself go a little weak inside in his presence. Martin slipped his hand into hers and pulled her on to the sofa. 'Now sit there whilst I get some coffee.'

Silently she nodded as she looked at Woody, who was joking about the sounds of the music booming out above them. Unzipping her case, Fran laid out her tape recorder beside her.

'Nervous?'

She looked up at the owlish glasses. 'You could say that,' she grinned.

'I'm just a person, for Christsakes. I've just eaten some pretzels for breakfast. How about you?'

There was no turning back, he had broken the ice. Martin brought in the coffee, although he was happily letting Woody do all the talking. Unconsciously she allowed herself to relax completely.

The interview went well, and after an hour of moods which veered from hilarity to melancholy, Fran knew in her heart that whatever happened now, Grace was going to be pleased.

The three of them took a taxi cab

to Central Park, then linking arms, and had an exhilarating walk in the warmth of the sun. Woody eventually kissed her cheek. 'You're a nice lady, I can tell.'

A warm glow stole over Fran at his directness. 'I'm very flattered, I've been a fan of yours for some time.'

'Then no doubt we'll meet again? You won't be able to stay away from New York.' He pecked her cheek again, slapped Martin on the arm, then was gone: lost in the lush greenery of the trees.

Martin turned her round to face him. 'Kiss me before I die of withdrawal symptoms.' Pulling her into the shade of a tree, she felt the jagged edges of the bark pierce her thin cotton dress, as he pressed himself against her body.

Fran sensed an urgency but also a special tenderness in his kiss that had been missing before. He held the nape of her neck in his long slender fingers, brushing his lips tenderly over her eyelids. In that magic moment, Fran felt her worries and fears about her future melt away in his kiss. Nothing mattered now except Martin.

'I've got something to tell you.' He uttered the words quietly, his cheek against her ear so that she couldn't see him. A sudden dread filled her at the tone of his voice. Intuitively she knew this was the end. He was going to leave her. 'I'm going away,' he continued.

She struggled to free herself, but he tightened his grip. She wanted to scream. Where to? For how long? Will you take me? But the words lodged in her throat and she pressed her lips together hard to stop herself from saying anything, or worse, crying. A voice inside her head was shouting, he's making a fool of you. But the other voice of reason was compelling her to listen hard and make sense of his words.

'It will be for a couple of months.'

'Why?' was all she could muster.

'It's a business . . . trip . . . '

'Come on, Martin.' Her voice was

stronger now. 'You can do better than that. You're a journalist like me, on a magazine. We don't get time off like . . . like . . . two months, unless . . . ' She stopped dead. 'Are you covering some war? No, you can't be. We're not that sort of magazine.'

Martin drove his hands through his hair and momentarily closed his eyes. 'Look, this isn't the place to discuss this.'

'It's as good a place as any.' She felt a little defiant now, but hated herself for doubting him.

'No, let's go back to the office.' He linked his arm chummily through hers, and dragged her back on to the path.

Once out of the park, as they drove along, her mind was in quiet turmoil. She was about to hear something ominous. Deep down, she knew it. Trying to rationalize didn't help. She had known Martin just seven days and yet her emotions felt exposed.

Mechanically she watched Martin paying the cab driver, and woodenly she walked towards the lobby. She felt his hand slip through hers. 'Angel, you go and do your articles on Woody.'

Blinking back the tears, she looked up at him. He wasn't going to tell her why he was going away. She willed herself to lift her head and steadily meet his gaze.

'All right,' she heard herself say. 'I'll do as you say.'

'I'll call later.' He looked past her head at the bustling street outside.

'Yes.' She tried to make her voice sound cheerful as she walked into the elevator. Together they stood in silence and he made no attempt to touch her as the light indicated the fourteenth floor. Briefly she turned and caught a look of tenderness on his face, then the bronze doors closed and Cassy's voice was calling her from across the deeply carpeted reception area.

'I don't want any calls,' Fran interrupted.

Cassy stood up and came round her desk. 'Hey . . . Heavy day huh! What about a pastrami on rye and coffee?'

Cassy's suggestion couldn't help but make Fran feel better. 'Wonderful.'

Cassy gave a curt nod of approval, and went out. Fran slumped into her chair, swivelling round so that she could see the skyscrapers. Briskly she sat up straight. Snap out of this, she reprimanded herself. There's a mountain of work, and tomorrow it wouldn't be him she'd be worrying about, but Grace.

She fed some paper into the typewriter, just as Cassy came in with her sandwich.

'I bought a mineral water too. OK?'

'Great,' Fran answered genuinely and bit into the sandwich.

Cassy looked pleased and left her to enjoy her lunch. Fran fought her gloom by concentrating on the sandwich. Then, clearing the debris, she began to write.

It was around 4.30 when Cassy came to see her. She poked her head round the door. 'Can I come in?'

'Yes, I could do with a break.'

'I don't suppose I'll see you again, but next year my sister and I want to visit England, can we look you up?'

Fran stood up, came round the desk, and gave her a squeeze. 'I'd love you to come and visit me. Stay for a few days, I've got an extra couple of bedrooms. Nothing special, but there's a welcome on the mat.'

Cassy kissed her cheek. 'I just knew you'd say that. It sure has been pleasant around here this past week. Have a pleasant flight, OK?' Cassy got to the door and turned. 'The calls will come direct through the phones, not through the switchboard.'

'Right,' Fran called as Cassy closed the door.

By six o'clock, the office was hushed and tranquil. Everyone had gone. Friday started the weekend for most New Yorkers, and it wasn't unusual for most workers to be out of their work by six. It came as a shock, therefore, when the phone rang.

It was the security guard.

'Hi Arnie.'

'Mr Bradly Wyatt told me to ring you and tell you to come up to his suite right away. It's the private elevator to the left of the stairs outside your office.'

Numbly she replaced the phone, and stood up in a daze. She had waited six days for this interview and she had dismissed the idea of ever seeing him in the flesh. Now, at the eleventh hour, he was asking her to go up to see him.

Snapping herself into action, she fumbled in her desk for the list of questions. She frantically brushed her hair, and took a hard look at herself in the mirror. Lipstick, she panicked, I need some lipstick. Her make-up bag fell on the floor in her hurry to get the small tube out. Then she took a deep breath to compose herself, and left the office.

Her heart fluttered in a most peculiar way as she watched the light in the elevator ascending as she reached the pinnacle of the building. The doors glided open and she stepped out to a large terrace surrounded by potted shrubs and flowers. It was a breathtaking sight against a canopy of stars, and all her fears fled in a moment of sheer wonderment at the beauty that faced her.

The whole of the terrace was enclosed by rounded glass, so no violent winds disarranged her hair. Intermingled with the potted palms were hanging baskets of flowers trailing swags of ivy. Drifting to the edge of the terrace to look down at the myriad twinkling lights that lit up the buildings, she wished with all her heart that Martin were here to share this moment.

Somewhere in the background music was playing, and turning she saw a shadowy figure watching her through the foliage from the room beyond.

Her heart skipped a beat, knowing that this was Bradly Wyatt. It took a great deal of her courage to walk towards him but she told herself that this was her mission fulfilled. This was it. The interview would be in the bag, in half an hour. Grace would be happy, she would be happy. She could relax and prepare to go back to London with contented heart.

He stepped closer and levered back the doors that separated his suite from the terrace. She took a small step forward and held out her hand. It was received by long slender fingers which made her freeze at their familiarity.

'Hello angel,' he said, lightening his grip on her hand.

'Martin,' she breathed, 'what are you doing up here? I've come to do the interview with Bradly Wyatt.'

'Yes, I know.' The voice was even and soft.

He moved out the shadows into the light of the lamplit terrace. She scanned his attire with surprise. He was dressed in an immaculate white tuxedo and dark trousers. His hair gleamed in the light and he smelt faintly of whisky. He pulled her towards him, and she let him kiss her. It was only when he had caressed her face and arms that she pulled back a little to look deeply into his eyes.

'What's wrong?' she asked, seeing his troubled look. There was a long pause.

'I've been trying to gather enough courage to tell you.' He glanced away. 'I live here . . . this is my home . . . '

It wouldn't penetrate. She stared up at him.

'I'm Bradly Wyatt.'

He had been loosely holding her hand, but with a suddenness which surprised him she wrenched herself free and ran towards the terrace. The elevator doors were firmly shut. He made no attempt to move.

'Let me out of here,' she hissed, framing herself against the terrace doors and the penthouse lounge. 'Let me out this minute!'

'Not until . . . ' he started.

'Let me out!' she screamed.

Swiftly he was beside her, covering her mouth with a firm hand. She flung herself sideways to escape the firm arms that had encircled her, but she hadn't reckoned with his strength. Tears spilled uncontrollably down her face.

'I want to go,' she sobbed. 'I want to go.'

'No . . . not like this. You're not going until I have told you about . . . '

She dropped her head, and put her hands over her ears. 'Liar, liar,' she breathed over and over again. 'Liar!'

'No.' He shook her hard, then grabbed her wrists and pulled her towards him, pushing her arms behind her so that she had no choice but to mould herself to him. He waited until she was calm, then he released her, one arm at a time, rocking her back and forth like a baby. 'I wanted to tell you, but it went on. In the end . . . I didn't know how to.'

'You could have told me,' she said miserably. 'You've been laughing at me.'

'Never,' he said with vehemence.

She had no alternative but to listen. He dabbed at her eyes and she let him wipe her tear-stained cheeks. Her resistance was melting with each passing second, even though her mind raced with questions.

He led her to the middle of the lounge where a sumptuous white leather sofa stood, and pulled her down beside him. 'Ever since I first saw you I wanted you.'

Sharply she turned, her anger mounting again. 'I'm not exactly Kim Basinger.'

'If I wanted her I could have her,' he answered nonchalantly. The blow she aimed at him caught him squarely on the cheek. He flinched then chuckled. 'I suppose that was deserved,' he said ruefully, rubbing his chin.

'You wanted a toy. You've had your fun, now let me out of here.'

He appeared to ignore her comments and walked to the bar. 'What will you have?' He held up a bottle and glass invitingly.

146

'Nothing.' She clenched her hands tightly together.

'I'll get you a vodka.'

'Do you hear right Martin . . . or do I call you Bradly?' Sarcasm shot across the room like a well-aimed arrow, and she knew by the look on his face, that it had found its target.

He put the bottle and glass on the bar, and walked towards her. 'Unfortunately, I had the advantage of you, I . . . '

'You can say that again,' she interrupted.

'Are you going to listen?' His voice had an edge to it. He waited until he saw a slight slump of her shoulders in resignation. 'When I realized where you'd come from, and that you were Grace's assistant, I knew from the first that you were Fran . . . '

'How could you?' she said with emotion. 'All the times we discussed Bradly Wyatt, and the interview.'

'I had to stall as long as I could.' He took a large gulp of his drink.

'Somehow I kinda suspected you would take it like this.' He sighed and walked over to step on to the terrace. He stared out across New York.

Fran stood up, putting the drink on the table. 'I'm sorry, I've got to go.'

They stood there, still in the half-light. Then he walked quickly to the bar. He must have pressed a button to open the elevator, because she saw a flood of light fill the terrace and light up the greenery and flowers on the terrace.

'So this is goodbye,' he said coldly, as though expecting rejection.

She felt a cold shiver shoot like a spasm through her rigid body. 'What do you expect?' Her voice felt stilted but she willed herself not to break down, here, in front of him.

She couldn't feel her feet as they dragged across the floor. All life seemed to have lost her body. She stood inside the brightly lit lift. It could have been her coffin. She felt dead.

Her last glimpse of Bradly was of

an austere, darkened figure gripping the polished ebony of the bar counter, before the doors slid shut. Although the elevator carried her body down, she had the sensation that her heart had been left in the penthouse.

She went straight to her office and cleared out her desk. Her typed articles were already neatly stacked in folders. She placed the articles and the small number of possessions in her executive case, then taking a considered glance round, she satisfied herself that she had everything. Her mind was made up. She was leaving New York tonight.

6

Fran walked to the desk and checked out.

Her taxi was waiting punctually, and she breathed a sigh of relief as she sped away towards John F. Kennedy airport. She glanced across at the vast New York skyline, and willed the tears not to fall as a tiny Statue of Liberty stood proud in the evening mist.

The red sky streaked dramatically behind the twinkling lights of the buildings, sending a pang of nostalgia shooting through her as she remembered how she and Bradly had stood against the rail. It had been the same kind of night and the memory hurt.

The glitzy airport swamped any thoughts she might have of the past, as she paid the driver. She wasn't looking forward to the next hour. Her ticket was for the morning flight, and she knew that she was going to have to use all her charm to try to get to London that night without a valid ticket. She was prepared to sit there all night, rather than go back to the hotel.

'Ma'am, can I help you?' A Pan Am steward studied her face.

'Yes . . . ' she stuttered slightly. 'I'm in a spot of trouble. I've got a ticket for the eight a.m. flight tomorrow.' Hurriedly she produced it. 'I want to go home now.'

'You're not having a good time.' He looked concerned.

'Not exactly. I'm here on business but some problems have arisen.'

'I see, and you're needed in London.' He looked at the destination on her ticket. She remained silent. He had drawn the wrong conclusion, but if it meant she could go back tonight, then she wasn't going to argue about it.

Efficiently, he took her ticket to the inner office. Within minutes he was back.

'No problems, we had someone cancel

their seat today for one tomorrow.'

Relief spread through Fran. 'What time is the flight?' she asked, keeping her voice calm.

'Two hours. You've got plenty of time to check in, get your duty frees ... ' Brightly he smiled at her, as he wrote out a new ticket. His friendliness cheered her. She had got what she wanted and within hours would be going to London.

If she hadn't felt so depressed, the prospect of seeing the old city again would have delighted her. As it was, her baggage felt like a lead weight as she pushed the trolley towards the check-out.

The bar was reasonably empty, so Fran bought a drink before settling down to wait. Her main aim had been to blot out her thoughts, but now, with nothing to occupy her, they flooded back like an avalanche. She clenched her jaws together and refused to cry.

With a pang she heard her flight being called. When the plane left the ground, it was already quite dark. Looking out, she saw thousands of lights. It reminded her of the tiny lights on the Christmas tree when she was small. The lights spread as far into the distance as the eye could see. It was then that she felt a tear trickle down, and the emotion sweep over her. She had fallen in love: in love with someone who had played a game with her. Fran wrenched her gaze away from the nostalgic scene.

The next hour was the worst in her whole life. She had to contend with the bustle and excitement of the other passengers, ordering drinks, talking about their trip to one another and generally enjoying themselves, while she endured the inner misery of unrequited love.

With a start, she heard the pilots' voice, telling the passengers that they would be in Heathrow in thirty minutes. In the dim light from the plane, she realized she had slept for practically five hours. Fran put it down to mental exhaustion, but was relieved that home was near.

★ ★ ★

The taxi turned off the Commercial Road, and drew to a halt outside her house. Nothing has changed, only me, she mused.

The first thing she did was to step out on to the patio. The shrubs seemed much thicker and taller. It felt good to be back, all of a sudden. She poked at some of the pots and realized that the earth was quite dry. The thought crossed her mind that the weather had been fine.

She busied herself for the next hour watering the shrubs. At the end of it she felt happier and, realizing how ravenous she now felt, cooked an omelette for herself. She was now wide awake, even though it was only seven in the morning.

She walked to the newsagent's and bought a newspaper. It was Saturday, and after browsing through the pages over another coffee, Fran decided that she was, after all, tired. She sat in the darkened bedroom, setting the alarm for two o'clock in the afternoon, having made up her mind to see Grace that very evening. It couldn't wait, and she had to recoup some of her lost energy before the confrontation that would be inevitable.

The continuous bleep of her alarm woke her up, but for a minute she was totally disorientated. Where was she? She could see a shape through the window. It wasn't a skyscraper. She was home in her own bed. The shape outside was the chimney on the roof opposite. For a minute she lay thinking of Bradly: the feel of his arms enveloping her body; his kisses, which were unforgettable and devastating. Then the tears fell, as she ached for him to be near.

Burying her head in the pillow, she sobbed hard for five minutes, then stopped as abruptly as she had started.

To go to Grace looking a puffy-eyed mess was unfair after the pain Grace had endured. She fought to control herself and momentarily won. A shower and hair-wash refreshed her; it was only in the stillness of the afternoon, when she was putting on her make-up, that she felt her lips quiver again at the realization that she would never feel Bradly's arms round her again.

Fran decided she wouldn't phone Grace and let her know she was coming. She didn't want to explain on the phone why she was back a day early. It was better face to face anyway. If she took a couple of steaks she was sure Grace could rustle up something for them.

Fran gulped as she stood on Grace's doorstep. Her boss was a great person, but how would she react to the news that Fran had bottled up inside her? A faintly queasy feeling hit her stomach as she wondered if she might even get the sack for failing to get a story that had been set up for her. It should have been the simplest job in the world, but it hadn't worked out, and now Fran was scared, for the first time in a week.

Mary, the housekeeper, beamed as soon as she saw Fran's familiar face.

'Who is it Mary?' Grace's voice called from the kitchen.

Fran put one finger across Mary's lips and walked down the hall.

'Mary . . . Fran . . . when?' Grace struggled to get out of her chair but her leg prevented her and she slumped back again. Fran bent and kissed her cheek then clung to her, as emotion and loneliness flooded her body.

'Honey, what's the matter?' Grace pushed her back gently, as Fran quietly let the tears spill down her cheeks. Grace hugged her, and stroked her hair as Fran knelt on the floor, her head in Grace's lap.

'Sit up on the chair and pour me a coffee,' she ordered in a firm but kindly voice. Fran obeyed without a murmur, then sat back in a chair opposite.

'OK. Spill the beans.'

'I'm scared,' Fran said bluntly.

'Of what, of whom?' Grace said directly.

'Of losing my job. Of what you might say.'

'I haven't heard what you've got to say yet and anyway, don't pre-empt my reaction to anything. I'm a Sagattarius you know; we're supposed to be a little philosophical.'

Fran smiled for the first time since she had arrived. 'Sorry Grace. I feel I've let you down badly. I've let the magazine down. And myself,' she added ruefully.

'Before we talk, are you going to stay for dinner?' Grace smiled at her. I don't deserve her, the thought crossed Fran's mind as she bent to pick up the plastic carrier bag.

'I bought a couple of steaks and a bottle. Will that do?'

'Marvellous. Mary's already made a cheesecake, and I've got the most marvellous piece of Stilton . . .'

'How's the leg.' Fran changed the subject.

'Getting along,' Grace answered, looking down at all the signatures scrawled across the white plaster. 'It wasn't a bad break, so they tell me, so this will be off in no time at all. I can't tell you how relieved I'll be.'

She looked over at Fran, who had quietened down. 'Mary, take these outside would you dear?' Grace called to Mary, who came in and took the bag from Grace. 'Fran, you open the wine, I haven't the strength, then we can talk.'

Grace suggested they sit on the terrace. It was still warm enough to sit out. Fran helped Grace get settled in a comfortable garden lounger.

'Don't you dare leave anything out,' Grace warned. 'I want . . . no . . . I think I deserve, the full account.'

'You don't have to say that Grace, I have every intention of telling you everything. It's where to begin.'

'Like the saying goes . . . at the beginning.'

Fran started slowly: recounting how she had met a man in a bookshop, accidentally, and how they had started dating almost at once; the fact that Bradly Wyatt was constantly putting off the interviews, and how worried she had become.

'But didn't you say over the phone that you had met Woody Allen?'

'Well . . . yes.'

'Then what the devil are you looking so glum about?'

'Because I didn't go out there for that, did I Grace?' Fran looked agitated. 'My brief was to get that interview with the elusive Bradly Wyatt.'

'So explain to me what happened when, say, Wednesday came, and he was still saying he was busy.'

'I hung around the office they gave me. He evidently doesn't like being interrupted, not even by his own staff in the building, so there was no way I could bump into him. Nor could I phone him and talk to him.'

'And then?' Grace leaned forward, interested.

'And then . . . Friday,' Fran sighed, 'I got the call to visit the penthouse. He lives at the top of the building in a penthouse.' Fran looked down as the memories came flooding back and shifted uneasily in her chair.

'Go on before I burst.' Grace smiled. 'You actually got up there. So what was the problem?'

'Before I tell you what happened up there, can I fill you in on the week?'

'You wrote some damn fine articles on New York I hope!'

'Yes, I did. It's a marvellous place and I hope when you read my articles you will like them, Grace. But I got involved with someone.'

'You mean love?' Grace beamed at her.

'I'm afraid so.' Fran felt the urge to cry again but kept control of the tears. This time she wanted to explain without losing her dignity.

'You don't look too happy about it. Doesn't he love you?'

'No,' Fran said boldly. 'No, he doesn't. In fact he was playing a game with me.'

'Typical,' Grace said sarcastically. 'There's always one in your life, and you had to meet him in New York. So tell me what happened.'

'We went everywhere. Saw all the most important sights. Being a New Yorker, he took me to little, out of the way places that the ordinary tourist wouldn't have known about. They would make good material for articles, so when I've got my act together, I'll be giving them to you.'

'Good. Good,' Grace said, with a hungry gleam in her eye. 'That November issue sounds as though it will work if you do a good job on your pieces. I can see it all now. Not the touristy stuff but the hideaways that the Americans relax in.'

'Yes, that's it. It was very exciting

Grace. I wouldn't have missed it for the world.'

'You see, even now you're being positive.' Grace smiled. 'Tell me about this guy.'

'He lived in Greenwich Village.'

'Wow.'

'In a dump. Spartan, not what you'd imagine,' Fran interrupted. Grace raised her eyebrows. 'Yes I'm telling you the truth. It was so bare and dull.'

'You could have made it homely if you'd have wanted to.'

There was a long silence.

'Grace, it was all an act. He didn't have to live like that. He had money. Lots of money. He took me there, to pretend he was someone else.'

'Sounds as if it worked,' Grace said quietly.

'Yes, it did. It did.' Fran cried. 'I thought he was a hard-up journalist . . . '

'Not the opposition?' Grace showed alarm on her face.

'No, he worked for our magazine.'

'So you were in the same building and . . . '

'Let me finish, Grace,' Fran pleaded. 'He took me out during the day. I wrote my articles, then dinner by candlelight in the evening. He cooked for me.'

'He wooed you. So how do you know he doesn't love you?'

Fran looked down at her knees. 'Friday, I was asked to see Bradly Wyatt . . . to do the interview . . . '

'Don't tell me. Your journalist friend got jealous.' Fran gave her a steady look.

'My journalist friend was up in the penthouse when I arrived.'

'He'd pipped you to the post and was going to do an article on Bradly Wyatt's wife?'

'Grace,' Fran said agitatedly. 'Grace . . . ' She grabbed her hand.

'What is it Fran? Now don't cry again.'

Fran took a handkerchief out of her handbag. 'Grace,' she said in a low voice. 'My journalist friend *was* Bradly Wyatt.'

It took Grace a few moments before she realized just what Fran had told her.

'You mean . . . Bradly had been taking you out, and you had no idea?'

Fran shook her head, her hair shielding her scalding face from Grace's sympathetic gaze.

'I'd never seen an actual picture of him, had I? There was no need. Funny,' she laughed through her tears, 'I'd even spoken to him on the phone. Quite a few times.'

'Yes, you had.'

'Messages when you were out', she looked across at Grace, 'but I never recognized his voice.'

'So you were called to the penthouse and he told you who he was.'

'Yes, and even when I saw my so-called journalist friend there in the penthouse, it still didn't click. What a fool he must have thought I was.'

'The flat in Greenwich?'

'Obviously he hired the set, so that the scene would be right,' Fran said bitterly. 'Martin, he called himself. What an idiot I am. He even arranged for me to meet Woody Allen. Funny, when your heart rules your head, you don't even question. How does a hack know a famous millionaire film star and scriptwriter so intimately, that he can, at the drop of a hat, arrange an interview for me, a mere nobody on a London magazine?'

'Stop it, stop it,' Grace said sharply. 'Stop wallowing in . . . in . . . '

'Self-pity,' Fran filled in heavily.

'Yes, and don't put words into my mouth.' There was an awkward silence for a few moments, and they both stared out at the swaying trees on the terrace.

'I mean,' Grace said in a low voice, 'I don't want to hear any more talk of you being a nobody. The magazine took you on because you had talent. I believe in you. The least you can do is believe in yourself.'

'I'm sorry Grace, I didn't realize. I'm feeling low and confused.'

'I'm sure you are.' The kind voice was back and Grace pulled herself up on her sticks. 'Let's go in. I'm ready for the steak.'

Later, when the wine bottle was empty, Grace leaned forward. 'You will spend tomorrow and Monday at home, going through your work. I'll see you Tuesday, perhaps Wednesday, to discuss the presentation. Thursday go to the photo library in Shelton Street and get a picture of Woody so that we can use it.'

'I did take some myself.'

Grace looked surprised, but pleased. 'Great, let's hope we can use them. Don't be surprised if Bradly calls me, will you? I'm the one he will turn to if he feels he has to.'

'Don't tell him I love him, will you?'

'Would I?' Grace asked innocently.

'If you thought it would make me happy, yes, I believe you would,' Fran said ruefully.

Grace laughed heartily. 'You're beginning to understand me. Let's take it as it comes, shall we? You concentrate wholly on getting those articles into tip-top condition. They've got to be good, then the whole trip will have justified itself even though we didn't get the interview.'

'Tell me something, Grace. Before I went you told me all about him. You said he used women, then abandoned them. But what I find particularly cruel is, that, right from the start, he knew who I was and the magazine I worked on.'

'I must admit, honey, I don't understand that bit either. I knew him as a lonely person who had been treated badly by his wife. I can't really put the same face on the man you have just described. He must have changed drastically.'

'The worst of it is, that he's still married. It hurts, Grace, whichever way you look at it.'

'I know, I know. Women live by their

emotions. Yes, they hold down better jobs than they've been used to, the law has seen to that, but deep down, Fran, we want love, lots of it, and we want it forever and ever, not just for five minutes. Even when we're having fun, we wonder if it will last.'

'Men are not the same, are they?'

'Thank God no.' Grace laughed. 'But we love 'em just the same. Although you've been through all this, you're not thinking evil thoughts about him. If he walked through that door now I know what you'd do,' Grace said directly.

'I hate him, Grace, for what he's done. I won't see him again. New York is in my past ... and if he walked through the door I'd throw your cheesecake at him.'

Grace laughed. 'No you wouldn't it's too good for that. Let's have some, shall we?'

Fran couldn't help smiling at her sense of humour. The woman had the ability to make her spirits soar and she knew why she'd made this her first call after the trauma of New York.

Later, when Grace hobbled to the front door, she gave her a warm hug. Fran clung to her as though she were her mother. The lump returned in her throat but she kept the tears at bay.

'Go home and try to get some sleep, Mary's called a taxi, it'll be here by now. Take it easy tomorrow. Cook yourself a breakfast, then work on your articles. I mean it. Work on a full stomach. See you when I see you. Just bring the work in when you feel you are ready.'

'Grace,' Fran choked, 'you are so kind to me.'

'Rubbish, you'll get the sack if they're not good enough.' Fran was gently pushed in the direction of the taxi.

She huddled in the dark of the cab, grateful that Grace lived only a stone's throw from her. She was tired, and was beginning to suffer the effects of jet lag.

It was raining when Fran woke up. The overcast sky didn't help her spirits but she took Grace's advice and downed some hot scrambled eggs and a mug of tea. She wandered to the patio and looked out, but the rain prevented her from pottering, as she normally would have done. She opened the door and stood breathing in the smell of fresh honeysuckle. What was Bradly doing now? Fran couldn't stop her thoughts drifting to the office building in New York. The penthouse would be in darkness now. The stars shining on the foliage on the terrace would be partly obscured by the glare of the reflected lights from the buildings.

What would Bradly be doing? The same recurring thought. Would he be in the penthouse or in the quiet of the flat in Greenwich?

Listlessly Fran turned. I've got to stop thinking: thinking is pain, she thought, grabbing her handkerchief and blowing her nose hard. The sight of her typewriter spurred her into action. The work she had done in New York lay at the bottom neatly stacked in folders.

Pulling them out, she studied each one, and started on the Statue of Liberty article. Many times, she was overwhelmed with memories and it was only with constant effort that she willed herself to go on until her arms ached and she could no longer think.

Grace had a meeting with the Editor in Chief. It was brief but informal.

'I take it I'll be seeing some of the New York articles very soon.'

He was a tall quiet man, but with a dynamism which had deceived many writers. He spoke quietly and had worked with Grace for ten years. She knew he always got what he wanted in the end but not without a certain amount of persistence. The kindly grey eyes were smiling at her.

'Fran's working on them right now so after I've checked them out we'll go over them.'

'I'm leaving it to you. I'm very keen to see what she made of the place. Fresh eyes and all that. No problems, are there?' he asked, seeing her hesitate.

'No . . . no, everything's fine.' Grace made her exit as soon as her coffee was finished.

If he scrutinized her any longer he'd drain the truth out of her. He had that kind of effect on people whilst hardly opening his mouth. It was 12.30 when for the umpteenth time she picked up the phone.

'Grace Black, *Charisma*.'

'Grace.' She knew as soon as the name was uttered, who it was.

'Bradly, how lovely to hear you again.' There was a slight pause as she gathered her wits about her. Grabbing a pen, she wrote his name idly on the pad in front of her.

'Grace, I have to talk to Fran.'

'She's not here,' Grace answered innocently. It wouldn't do to let him know she knew too much yet.

'When will she be back, after lunch?'

'No, I've given her a few days off to get her articles into shape. She'll be here on Wednesday.'

'Damn,' she heard him curse.

'How's things?' she shot out a probe.

'Lousy. Look, I'm thinking of coming over. There's some business in London next week.'

Grace felt elated for some reason. 'Wednesday, why don't you come here for dinner?'

'Splendid, and Grace . . . you'd better not tell anybody of my arrival. It's not a time-and-motion study of the London office.'

Long after Bradly had rung off, Grace sat thoughtfully looking down at the phone. In her heart, she knew there was going to be a confrontation. There was no way that true love could be kept apart, and Fran would need all the help and support that she could give her.

7

Fran had a leaden feeling inside as she walked into the office the following Wednesday. She remembered how, only days earlier, she had walked down Lexington to Bradly's penthouse suite. She knew she'd never see him again and she didn't think she'd ever get over him. Bradly's lean dark features filled her thoughts and mind as she stood in the lift.

Would she ever get the chance of such happiness again in her life? The answer was a loud denial in her head as the doors slid open. What use was her cosy little house if it was constantly empty? There'd never be another Bradly. She pictured him in the club he had taken her to, in the battered leather armchair, and looking immaculate in his evening clothes on the terrace of the penthouse. Her eyes brimmed with tears as she pushed open the door of her office.

There was a ghostly quiet and strangeness about it. Vacantly she stared at the street below, her thoughts continents away. Grace hobbled in five minutes later.

'Earlybird,' she hailed. 'Couldn't you sleep?'

'I wanted to get back.' Fran ignored the latter remark.

She hadn't slept a wink but she was determined not to bother Grace any more with the problem of Bradly. Work was going to solve her problem, and no amount of consoling words would heal her wounds. She had wanted to get away from everybody, disappear, so that she wouldn't have to talk. But with the dawn, after a sleepless night, the answer was obvious. By six she had eaten breakfast and had walked down empty streets.

'I've got the articles here.'

'Good, give me ten minutes to look at the mail, then we can get our heads down.'

Grace noticed the dark circles under Fran's eyes but kept silent. 'Get some coffee on the go,' she called over, attacking the envelopes of the morning's mail with ferocious delight.

Busying herself with the coffee gave Fran a chance to stop thinking of herself. 'How's the leg?'

'I may not make the first eleven yet, but I'm getting there.' Grace, cheerful as ever, pushed the letters to one side and took the coffee Fran offered her. 'Now, what have we got here?' She looked with interest at the files that Fran had placed on her desk.

The phone rang, and Grace made a grab for hers simultaneously with Fran. Fran got there first.

'*Charisma* magazine. Assistant Features Editor speaking.'

Grace drew her breath in, waiting for Fran to tell her it was Bradly on the phone. Fran wrote 'Features Editor' on a pad and Grace wrote back 'not in yet'.

'I'm afraid she's not arrived yet, try in half an hour.'

They spent the morning reading articles together, and being constantly interrupted by the phone. Each time it rang, Grace felt her heart skip a beat. When the call did come, Grace was out of the room.

'*Charisma*,' Fran said lightly. There was a brief silence, then a click as the phone was replaced. With a shrug Fran resumed her work.

'Who was that?' Grace hobbled back quickly into the room.

'Nobody, they hung up.'

Grace knew instinctively it had been Bradly and that he would phone again. 'Fran, how about getting some sandwiches? I'm famished.'

'Same as usual?' Fran raised her eyebrows.

'I like tuna,' Grace said emphatically, smiling.

Grace waited for the phone to ring when Fran had gone. She was not disappointed. Bradly had stood beside the phone at Heathrow prepared to put every last ten-pence in the phone until Grace answered.

'Grace.'

'Bradly, where . . . Heathrow? No, you're not going to the Hilton, you're staying with me. No arguments, I insist.'

Bradly hesitated, then agreed. 'I won't be in the way?'

'Were you ever? Mary will let you in. Anyway, it's time we had a talk.'

She waited for him to answer. He had the power to say whatever he liked to her. But all she heard was a deep resigned sigh as he muttered, 'Yes, I'd like that,' before he rang off.

Grace looked up as Fran appeared with the sandwiches. 'Come round for drinks on Saturday? I'm having a few people in.'

'Birthday?' Fran asked with a smile.

'I never have them,' Grace hurled at her. 'No, just a get-together.'

Hours later, Grace flung down her pen. 'Right, I've had enough.' Grabbing her stick, she let Fran help her to the lift. She turned to look at her younger companion. 'How do you feel now?'

Listlessly Fran answered, 'I've got my life to lead, he's got his. I'm sorry our paths crossed.'

'Don't talk rubbish, you're glad you met him, and I'll call you a liar if you say otherwise.'

Fran shrugged and turned her head away, stifling the tears that threatened. 'I've got to put him into the past, Grace, or I'll go mad. All my energy now must go into my work.'

'Like a sort of nun,' Grace said, straightfaced.

Fran knew Grace was trying to be funny, but she didn't laugh. There was a small awkward silence. 'I think you can manage without me. I'll see you tomorrow.'

Grace said nothing as she pressed the button for the ground floor. It was a tactless thing to say to someone so vulnerable. The usual taxi that took her home only stopped once.

'You'll soon do without me,' the driver said cheerfully as he helped her out of the cab.

'I sincerely hope so, I don't think I can take any more of your jokes,' Grace laughed.

Mary told her Bradly was in the lounge as soon as she opened the door. At that moment Bradly emerged, tall and very dark. She sensed a fragile boyishness about him as he clung to her. He could have been her own child, she thought, as she saw the desperate look on his face.

'Tell me all about it in the kitchen. Tea is my most immediate thought.'

He laughed. 'You don't change a bit, do you, Grace?'

Skilfully he hoisted her to him with one arm to speed her progress to the kitchen. When tea was made she sat down opposite him.

'What would Jack have said?' she asked him as he finished the story.

'He'd say I was an idiot.'

'No,' Grace said slowly. 'You haven't

done anything idiotic yet.'

'There's still time?' His glum smile disturbed her.

'Look. You come and go from here as you please, but don't come to the office. On Saturday I'm having a get-together; Fran will have calmed down a bit by then.'

'How is she?' The words hung in the air.

'She's a woman,' Grace said intently. 'How do you think she is?'

Bradly said nothing. 'I've got to do a few talks in Europe next week. I won't be here again for at least six weeks. What am I going to do Grace?' He looked morosely into his tea.

'You could have any woman in the world Bradly,' Grace said quietly. 'What do you want from Fran?'

'I love her,' he said simply.

'Well you'd better be sure about it, before you break her heart a second time. If you're lucky enough to get the chance that is. Look, I've an idea. Why don't you take Fran as your assistant to Europe?'

Bradly's eyes gleamed with interest, but he looked dubious. 'Would she come?'

'She'd have to, or lose her job — you're the boss.'

'She might just leave.'

'No, she's too keen to get into print and stay there. I'd bet my housekeeper, she'd . . . well, perhaps not my housekeeper,' Grace said thoughtfully. 'She won't leave. But it may not be the simplest job in the world persuading her to accompany you.'

'You're brilliant. Why didn't I think of it before?' He walked over to her and gave her a hug.

'Hey don't get excited, she's got a mind of her own, you know.'

'What could she do?' He looked puzzled.

'Women are creative thinkers, Bradly, I've said it before. She could invent a sick aunt and ask for time off.'

Bradly sat down. 'We couldn't stop her either.'

'Or challenge her story without upsetting her again,' Grace added quickly. 'How are you getting to Europe?'

'Heathrow to Paris, Venice and finally back to New York.'

'Take her, and if she doesn't fall in love with you all over again then you'll never get her. I warn you though, it won't be a pushover. You've hurt her by not telling her who you were in the first place.'

'Why, for God's sake?' he demanded.

'She thinks you were having a game with her.'

Bradly smacked his fist into the open palm of his other hand in frustration.

'Getting down to more practical matters. When is the flight at Heathrow?'

'Sunday. Ten in the morning.'

'Be at my party on Saturday.'

'No, Grace. I think maybe we'll keep it on a business level at first, or she'll never get on the plane.'

'You're right. Mary!' she bawled.

Mary came in. 'Dinner is all ready. I was waiting for you.'

Grace looked at Bradly. 'You can see why I wouldn't bet my housekeeper. What a gem.'

They went into the lounge, where Mary had laid out a beautiful table: salad in a glass dish, apple pie on a silver tray and candles glimmering on the lace cloth, lighting the whole.

'I brought you some of your favourite wine — Saint Emilion.' He handed her the bottle as she sat down.

'You open it. I think I'm going to enjoy this,' she said, smiling happily at him.

'I'll bring you more than a bottle if your idea works.'

'And the sack if it doesn't.'

Hours later she sat alone in the lounge listening to the rain beat down outside, wondering about the delicate business of getting Fran to go off for six weeks on a trip to Europe.

By the time Friday had arrived, the

articles Fran had written had all been revised and finished. Grace, unusually, shut the door of her office as Fran walked in with her usual coffee.

'Charlie, I don't want any callers put through for half an hour. OK?'

Fran wondered what on earth she was going to say.

'I'll come straight to the point Fran. How do you feel about accompanying an author on a book promotion?'

'As what?' Fran asked innocently.

'Assistant, helper, glorified secretary-cum-organizer. You've probably done something like it before.'

'It'd be fantastic. Where's he going?'

'Paris, book fair; Venice, lectures and book fair. It will be hard work. But it would be an interesting experience for you. Might even get some writing out of it.' Grace waited, praying silently.

'Why me?'

'He's a friend of mine, he wanted a competent assistant. I recommended you.'

'How will you manage?'

'Like I did when you were in New York.' She laughed. 'No, this time I've got an experienced temp.'

'Got!' Fran's eyes widened. 'You predicated my answer?'

'You won't turn down an opportunity to write a few articles first-hand about the book fairs. You're too ambitious for yourself.'

'When do I go.'

'Sunday; you'd better pack tonight. You'll have a modest expense account so don't worry if you haven't time to shop.'

'Saturday's going to be frantic.' They laughed together.

'Don't forget my party. Stay a little sober, the flight is at ten. A car will pick you up at 8.30, so you won't have that worry. Now you'd better be off and do some packing. And Fran . . .'

'Yes?' Fran turned, her fingers still on the door-knob.

'Just remember that whatever happens, you're doing this for me. I want you to go,' she said forcefully.

Fran stammered slightly at Grace's vehemence. 'OK . . . ' she said nervously.

'Just remember.' Grace's words hung in the air long after she had left the building.

Still puzzled, she wandered round the patio. The smell after the previous evening's rain was lush and pleasant to her nostrils and she breathed in the fragrance of the honeysuckle. She'd give Grace her key. There may not be any rain for a month, and the garden would be dead when she got back. Walking into the kitchen, she made a note on top of a pad. 'Plants, Grace, key.'

It took quite a while to pack, but Grace had given her a short itinerary. Perplexed, she stared down at it. Light business suits, some evening wear, not too formal, swimwear. 'Swimwear?' she said aloud. What on earth would she want with that on a business trip? Her bikinis were thrown into the case. No, she decided mentally, much too revealing. She'd take a couple of smart one-piece swimsuits. It wouldn't be right to give this author the wrong idea.

By four on Saturday, she was glad that she could slump down on the patio and sip a cool drink. The case was packed and standing in the hall: passport and money all ready. Impulsively she had splashed out and bought a red linen classic shirtwaister dress which she thought might look good to travel in. At least the author would recognize her. She stared at a ginger cat picking its way along the greenhouse roof and wondered what her travelling companion would be like. Probably a bespectacled intellectual, she mused. Lucky devil, getting his books into print.

After a leisurely bath, she took down a soft peach silk dress which looked stunning against her heavy auburn hair. Many people complimented her in glowing terms on her arrival.

'Where's Grace?' Fran searched the

crowded hallway. 'You'd better get rid of this.' Fran thrust a bottle of Beaujolais into Mary's hands.

'Darling.' Grace kissed her on both cheeks and pulled her towards a woman in a smart black trouser suit. 'Meet Sarah Milton.'

Startled, Fran gazed at her. '*The Sarah Milton*?'

'I'm afraid so. Am I a disapointment?' The woman oozed charm and warmth as she held out her hand to Fran.

'I'm so pleased to meet you, I've read so much of your work.'

'I'll leave you two if you don't mind.'

Fran turned again to the writer. 'Tell me how you started writing.' She sipped her drink.

'Well, it's rather a long story.'

They shuffled slowly through the throng until they reached the window seat overlooking the square. The next hour went quickly as Fran listened intently to the writer.

'If you had to pick out one tip to

potential writers, what would it be?'
Fran studied the clear features of the
woman opposite.

Thoughtfully, Sarah Milton looked
away, then back at Fran. 'Markets,'
she said simply. 'Know who you are
aiming at, and make yourself aware
very thoroughly, of what your readers
want. If you misjudge it, you won't get
printed.' She shrugged in a knowing
way.

'I'm sure there are a lot of people
here who are waiting to talk to you,'
said Fran, taking her leave of the
author.

They shook hands again and Fran
mingled back in the throng of people
in the room. There seemed to be a
distinct lack of air and she, eventually
got out into the garden. The warm
evening air felt like an aphrodisiac
as she breathed deeply. The scent
of honeysuckle filled the air, as she
walked further into the shadows of
the huge apple tree. There were no
lights in the garden, so no guests had

wandered on to the patio, even though the evening was warm and balmy. She felt herself swaying slightly and leaned against the garden shed behind the tree. Too much drink, she told herself, as she felt herself being held firmly against the door.

Fran couldn't see in the dark who was there. 'Thanks,' she said huskily, 'I seem to be a little unsteady.'

The man came closer, and moulded himself against her. A warmth flooded through her as the musky scent of him filled the air. A voice in her was telling herself not to be a fool. The other was telling her this was a party. She was a free agent. She had no ties. He bent his head and kissed her gently on the lips, just as she remembered Bradly did.

'Bradly,' she murmured as her lips parted. He brushed his lips over hers and for one frozen moment she was gripped with fear. She pushed at the man's chest but he was too strong for her. She couldn't see him, but the fragrance of his cologne seemed all too familiar. It was Bradly! Suddenly she was alert.

He crushed her lips to his in a passionate, devouring embrace. She tried hard to push him away, but found herself responding to his kiss with every passing second.

'It's you!' she hissed. 'It's you.'

'Yes, my darling, its me.' He laughed gently. 'What are you going to do about it?'

'Let me go, or I'll scream the place down.' In the darkness she felt flushed and hot, but this only served to excite him, as he bent again and felt her cheek.

'You won't scream, because you won't want to draw attention to yourself.'

'So sure of yourself, aren't you?'

'No,' he said slowly, 'but I'm sure that you don't mind me holding you like this.'

'So wrong,' she whispered loudly. 'How can anyone be so wrong about somebody? I don't want you ever to touch me again.'

'But what will we do for the next six weeks?' he murmured softly.

'Well I don't know about you, but I'm fortunate enough to be going to Europe with an author. Since you own the magazine, you ought to know that.'

She moved slightly but he shifted his leg so that she still felt pinned to the wall, like a butterfly that had lost its wings. 'Yes, I do know that.'

There was a long silence in which neither of them spoke. She felt him looking intently into her face, even though she could only see the outline of his head. The full moon had slipped from behind the cloud where it had lain hidden and in the soft but stark light they could now see each other very clearly. All the old feelings flooded back as his strong dark features came into view. But she had been hurt and her emotions were in a fragile state. This was the man who had tricked her into a relationship. Film stars and models fell at his feet. He didn't want her, she was sure of that, but only needed her for his own ends.

Fran was suddenly aware that Bradly knew more about her trip to Europe than he was saying. 'I'm flying tomorrow.'

'Yes, I know that too.'

She began to feel decidedly uncomfortable. Exasperated by his quiet control she defiantly lifted her head to ask him the author's name. But he took this as a provocative flirtatious invitation on her part and bent his head to kiss her once more. As the wave of passion melted her innermost resistance he whispered in her ear. 'You're coming with me Fran, I'm the author.'

With a shudder she broke free and stumbled against the roots of the tree as she tried to run. He caught her and pulled her up, as she struggled to contain her emotion.

'No,' she cried softly. 'You can't do this to me.'

'Listen to me.' He shook her hard. 'I need you as an assistant.'

'Don't take me. There are hundreds you could take.' She fought back the tears as her voice broke.

'How ambitious are you? Do you want to write or are you going to let your emotions get in the way of your work?'

She slumped as his hands held on to her shoulders. 'Do you always treat your employees as though you own them?' She resigned herself to the power she knew he had to destroy her. 'I'll leave if you don't mind,' she said stiffening.

'My car will take you home.'

'If I had bleeding feet I'd walk rather than let you drive me home.' She tossed her head. 'Anyway, my home is my castle.' Her eyes bored through him, and she gathered strength from the hurt look on his face, but it didn't stop her blushing. She wasn't naturally callous, but she wanted somehow to get her own back.

She heard Grace calling from the garden.

'I'm here,' she answered, wiping quickly at a tear that lay on her cheek.

Bradly came out of the shadows and Grace looked genuinely surprised. Fran watched her carefully, knowing she had arranged the trip to Europe. 'Bradly.'

'I couldn't keep away.'

Grace looked sharply at Fran.

'I know all about it.' Fran quivered and tried to walk past Grace.

'Fran,' Grace pleaded. 'Don't be upset with me.'

'What do you expect? Is everyone intent on fooling me? At least I won't have to wear my new red dress so that he recognizes me,' she flung over her shoulder as she entered the kitchen.

'Let her go,' Bradly said quietly. 'She'll be there tomorrow.'

'Will she ever forgive me?' Grace's usual sparkle slightly deflated, she took Bradly's hand and led him towards the lighted house.

'I'd better be going. She won't let me drive her home.'

'She's very independent.'

'Don't I know it? Little vixen. It'll be a challenge to take her in hand.'

Grace threw back her head and laughed. 'Good luck. Just make sure you want her, she's all heart.'

Bradly gave Grace a brief look, then bent and kissed her on the forehead. 'Take care,' he said, striding manfully out through the crowd, leaving Grace wondering if this trip would achieve anything.

Fran sat on the darkened patio sipping some coffee, staring up at the stars. Her heart skipped a beat every time she thought about her meeting with Bradly. He was here in London. Not just for her, though, she thought. He was here for the book and the European tour. Her jaw tightened. OK, she'd go. But she wouldn't be at his beck and call. She'd go and do her job because she was good at it. Better than most she thought, remembering some of Grace's compliments. But if he wanted her to accompany him in the evenings, she'd make sure she just wasn't available.

'I'm not going to let him hurt me again,' she murmured out loud.

'Oh yes, you will,' the voice in her head that wouldn't be silenced sang softly.

8

Sinking back into the taxi, the deserted roads flashing past, Fran tried to repress the queasy lurches in her stomach. The headiness of the party wine had long gone with the black coffee and a good night's sleep. Now the empty streets of Sunday in London, early in the morning, gave her a clear head.

She was wearing, after much internal debate, the red dress: partly because she wanted to look smart and efficient, but also because she could not deny that she looked good in red, and that she would be seeing Bradly again.

It wasn't difficult to spot him. In a cream suit, he stood out in the crowd of tourists. He hadn't seen her as she approached, her heart pounding erratically.

'Hello.'

'You made it then.' He tried to

sound casual and warm, but she could sense that for once, he was unsure of himself, and of her reaction.

'I'm always punctual,' she said demurely.

'Over here.' Bradly led the way to the first-class desk.

'Have you an itinerary?' she asked briskly.

He felt in his inside pocket and handed it to her. 'I've been carrying this one around, but I've got a decent one in my briefcase, in slightly better condition.'

She kept her face immobile, and looked down at the crumpled piece of paper. Her eyes widened as she saw the cities. 'Then we really are going to Paris?'

'Yes, then Venice. The others are just small towns.'

She read on, and he glanced over her shoulder. 'Metropole in Venice is right opposite St George's Island.'

She couldn't help a tremor of excitement flowing through her body.

The Metropole was famous for its comfort and cuisine. She knew that for as long as she lived she'd never get the chance to stay in a hotel like that again. But the bubbling excitement was quoshed when she saw his boyish grin. What was he gloating about? The fact that he'd got her here, against her will?

'Paris first then; when do we arrive?'

'About twelve, possibly one, by the time we've cleared Customs.'

He pushed their cases through the baggage control and took her arm. She stiffened and, unsuccessfully, tried to shrug him off. He propelled her towards Passport Control, where a number of policemen combed through the faces of the crowd.

'Would you like coffee?'

'No,' she said immediately, anticipating his offer. 'I'm going to buy some magazines.'

She left him standing amongst the cameras and souvenirs of the duty-free shop, and sped away. Quite suddenly, she felt light and happy. She was going to Europe and she felt in complete control. Idly she wandered over to the perfume counter at the edge of the duty-free lounge. She dabbed some expensive perfume on her wrists and throat.

'Would you like some perfume?' Bradly's voice whispered in her ear, jolting her back to the present.

'Not from you Bradly,' she murmured quietly.

'Did you get your magazines?' he asked, ignoring her snub.

'No, as a matter of fact, I came back to get the flight number.'

He laughed richly. 'There, you see, you do need me after all.'

'Just give me the flight number, so that I can watch the time on the monitors,' she said sweetly.

He handed her the paper. 'We haven't got long,' he called as she walked away.

Fran didn't turn, but kept walking. Having bought her books, she settled in the lounge, where she could keep an eye on the flashing digits on the screen above her. From time to time, she saw Bradly anxiously scouring the lounge with his eyes. 'Let him worry,' she muttered, keeping her head immersed in her magazine. He'd have her company soon enough on the flight to Paris.

The flight turned out to be uneventful, and although they were travelling in first-class luxury, it didn't stop the tension. She felt his body sink down beside her in the comfortable seat.

'What did you think of the meal?' he asked politely.

'I've never eaten off real china in an aircraft before. It makes a pleasant change.' Fran kept her voice deliberately cool but civil, then turned her head away from him to look at the scene of Paris below her. It would be a relief to get away on her own.

As if sensing her coldness towards him, he made no more effort than was necessary to converse with her until they reached the hotel.

Stony-faced, he stood beside her at the reception desk. 'I've booked rooms 201 and 202,' he said curtly.

'*Oui Monsieur.*' The receptionist gave him the keys and Bradly promptly turned and handed one to the porter.

'The porter will see you to your room, I've some friends to visit. Don't wait for me for dinner.'

Numbed by his obvious change of attitude she followed the porter, who had stepped smartly forward and picked up her cases. The last glimpse she had of Bradly was of him smiling with the elegant receptionist. He was in the process of handing back his room keys. The lift doors closed, leaving her with an emptiness which wouldn't go away.

The porter swung open the pastel-pink door to room 202. She gasped at the sheer beauty of it. She walked, ankle-deep in champagne-coloured carpet, towards the windows as if in a dream. All the antagonism of the flight was dispelled as she glanced out of the windows down at the Champs Elysées and the Parisians, still shopping.

The beige satin duvet on the bed looked warm and inviting, and before she could change her mind she had stripped off and was wallowing in a bubbly bath. The towels were soft and luxurious and when she was dried she slipped the duvet over her, smiling as she fell back into a much-needed sleep.

It was already dark when she awoke. The honking of horns outside in the street reminded her of where she was. She had been to Paris before when she had been to college. She donned some jeans and a thick jumper. She would eat in the French Quarter at Jacques' restaurant. Locking the door she started to bound down the stairs, avoiding the lift.

'Where d'you think you're going?' Bradly's voice rang through her, making her freeze. Her heart was pounding like this before.

'Well? . . . Paris isn't exactly like London, you know. Some areas are quite dangerous.'

'That didn't seem to worry you when you left me to my own devices earlier,' she said, recovering her poise. 'Why did you come back?'

'I thought I'd better take you to dinner.'

'No thanks.' She tried to rush past him but he shot out his arm and grabbed her waist, holding her firmly.

'Where were you going dressed like that?'

'A place I know,' she replied distantly.

'Then I'll come too.'

'Not in those clothes.' She couldn't help giggling now. 'They'd throw you out.' She leaned back on the balustrade, away from the warmth of his arm.

'Come back with me and wait whilst I change,' he pleaded. They stared at one another and she felt a pang of guilt at the way she had treated him.

'OK,' she said quietly. 'But I warn you, it's not fancy. I stayed here sometimes in my student days, and ate at Jacques' when I could afford it.'

'Then I'll love it.' He smiled openly now at her.

Reluctantly she climbed the stairs again and waited for him to unlock his door. Her heart beat faster as she entered.

'You sit there whilst I shower.' He sat her down on the bed.

She waited until he had gone into the bathroom before shifting herself on to a chair by the window. She wasn't going to be compromised again by him. He had cast a spell over her in New York, but she'd make quite sure he didn't do it again. She tussled with herself, debating whether to run out now and leave him to eat alone. She stood up and walked to the door. At the moment, Bradly opened the door of the bathroom.

'Don't be shy, I've got a robe on,' he chuckled.

'I can see that.' She stared at the

glistening black hair, trying to still her thumping heart.

Lithely he walked in the opposite direction to the wardrobe and got out a pair of check trousers and a thin black sweater. She could see the muscles of his chest rising and falling as he stood pulling it down over his head in front of her. The sight of him brought memories flooding back and she got up and looked out at the street to hide her face lest he should see the desire she felt.

'Let's eat shall we?' he said.

The French Quarter was crowded as usual as they picked their way past the small cafes and restaurants.

'How long is it since you've been here?'

'Five years.'

'It might have closed down,' he suggested.

'Never. Jacques and his family had this passed to him by his father and his father, and his father,' she said as they turned a corner and looked up at the name over the door. 'It just would not close down. Not ever.' She said belligerently.

'Point taken.' He smiled. 'There is an obligation to keep the family line going then?'

'They are very proud of their sons.'

Jacques was standing with his back to the door as they entered, but his wife shouted out. 'Francesca? Is it my little Francesca? It's been so long!'

Jacques spun round, wide-eyed, fixing her with his large brown eyes. Growling, he pushed his way through the crowded restaurant.

'Jacques,' she said, hugging him affectionately.

Madeleine, his wife, was beside him now and she kissed Fran on both cheeks, her eyes flashing past to look at Bradly.

'This is Bradly Wyatt, a friend of mine.'

'You're not married then?' Madeleine said bluntly, looking first at one, then the other.

Bradly laughed but took advantage of the mistake to slip his arm round Fran's waist. Fran flushed at the movement. Madeleine would take it as a sign that they were engaged, and it infuriated her that Bradly should, once again, get it all his own way.

'Shall we sit down?' She looked up at Bradly.

'Whenever you like,' he said, looking deeply into her eyes. She felt her heart begin to throb.

Jacques laid before them a simple *bouillabaisse* with chunks of garlic bread, and a bottle of Muscadet. He hovered for a moment beside the table. 'Olivier is home.'

'Good, then maybe we could offer him some wine.'

Bradly cordially lifted the glass and stared at Fran and then at Jacques. Jacques drifted away, leaving an awkward silence. 'Do tell me about Olivier,' Bradly said casually, pouring her some more wine.

'Don't spoil the meal, Jacques makes

the best *bouillabaisse* this side of Mareseilles. You'll meet Olivier soon enough.'

Bradly took a deep breath, just as the door opened and a slim dark young man came in with two friends. Immediately Fran waved to him and he rushed over and hugged her. 'I'm here on a short visit,' she explained.

Bradly pulled a chair over and beckoned the waiter for another glass. The men shook hands formally eyeing each other as strangers do when a mutual woman friend is present.

'This is my boss,' Fran said curtly, introducing them to each other.

Bradly looked visibly annoyed at the way Fran had described him, but Olivier didn't seem to notice. He clinked his glass, however, in a convivial gesture.

'Your father's food is superb. I take it you'll be entering the family profession too?'

'Good heavens, no.' Olivier grimaced. 'I'm going to be a musician.'

'Who will carry on the business?' Bradly asked.

'Louis is very keen. He's even learning the trade at college,' Olivier chuckled softly. 'But Jacques thinks the eldest son should take over, even though there are two other brothers.'

'It's best you make your own decisions in life.' Olivier looked at them both.

'My father insisted I learn his trade,' Bradly continued quietly.

'And you regretted it?'

'No, I made some good friends, I'm surrounded by most things I like. And I make a good living.'

'Are you happy though?' Olivier persisted.

'I wasn't at first, now I am. I've developed the business in my own way.'

'Are you trying to tell me to give up my music?' Olivier's hand paused as he lifted his glass.

'No,' Bradly said in a determined voice. 'But why not combine your music with this family restaurant? It doesn't have to be solely as Grandfather Jacques envisiaged it, does it?'

For a full minute, Olivier stared hard at Bradly, then threw back his head and laughed. He drained his glass and stood up. 'I believe, my friend, you have just made my father a very happy man.'

He pushed back his chair, and Madeleine and Jacques looked slightly perplexed as Olivier made his way over to them, put his arms round his father and gave him a hug. Jacques said something to him, and Olivier then grabbed his mother and all three of them bent their heads in a small huddle.

Fran and Bradly watched as Madeleine, tears streaming down her face, tenderly kissed her son. Jacques gave his son another quick hard hug, before making his way towards their table. His voice cracking with emotion. He shook Bradly's hand.

'*Mon ami*, can I ever thank you enough.'

Bradly waved his hand. 'The truth coming from someone else, is sometimes more palatable. He can't give up his music. This way he won't have to. Long after you have retired, his sons might be trying to turn this back into a restaurant, without the music.'

Jacques roared with laughter at the suggestion, then, looking at Fran, said softly, 'Your friend. I like him. You should hang on to such wisdom.'

Fran smiled at Jacques and cast a tentative look at Bradly.

'He's right of course,' Bradly answered boldly.

Fran snorted as Jacques ordered champagne for all the customers.

On the way home as they stood looking at the lights dancing on the Seine, a nostalgia crept over Fran as she remembered the last time that they had stood together in New York looking over the East River. Why had he behaved so badly towards her? Pretending that he was a regular guy from the Village, when he probably had two or three houses scattered about the world. She'd never fathom him out.

'What are you thinking?' he asked quietly.

'Nothing much, just how beautiful the Seine is.' She didn't turn, but was aware that he wasn't trying to touch her. 'It's late, and we have a book fair tomorrow. Shall we get a taxi?'

He took the hint and stayed withdrawn and reticent until they reached their rooms. 'Can I offer you coffee?'

'I don't think so,' she said briskly, pushing her key into the lock.

Then, before she could move, he had spun her round and pulled her into his arms. At first she resisted, but the combination of the champagne and the wine, left her with no strength to defend herself. He must have felt her limpness, and held her away from him, smiling down at her closed lids.

'Shall I see you to bed?'

His words shocked her into action and with one movement, she had turned the key and was in the room, slamming the door firmly. Panting for breath she felt the coolness of the door against her shoulder-blades.

'Pig,' she cried gently as a tear rolled down her cheek.

Sleep did not come easily although she felt fuzzy. She imagined she could hear music playing somewhere near.

There was a strained atmosphere at breakfast, only relieved by the quality of the hot croissants and coffee. Both were delicious and Fran remarked on them more than once. She looked smart in a dog-tooth black and white suit.

'You're looking very lovely today,' he said without sentimentality.

'Thank you. Have you today's itinerary?' She was trying hard to avoid acknowledging his compliments, but couldn't help quiet pleasure stealing over her.

'It's in my room, I usually start the day with breakfast, not business. I know that's unfashionable these days.'

A faint air of sarcasm crept into his voice but his tone was pleasant and inoffensive.

'Sorry, we've a lot to get through, and I've not really done anything like this before.'

'From what I've heard, you are super-efficient. What more could I ask for, from an assistant?'

She stared hard into his eyes, but had to look away in the end. He could outstare the devil, she thought cynically. They left the dining-room, the aroma of fresh coffee still in the air as they climbed the stairs, avoiding the lift.

'You can look at the itinerary now, if you like,' he said, pausing with his hand on the handle to his room. She faltered. This was the second time he had invited her into his room, but she had to see the itinerary and set her mind at rest.

The room smelt of shaving soap, clean and fresh. She waited whilst he fumbled in his briefcase to get the papers. Fran sat by the window, her figure outlined by the bright sunshine that pierced the lace at the window. He sprawled across the duvet, watching her read. She was acutely aware of the body slumped on the bed, and the fact that she was in his domain. He moved and she sprang like a cat, knocking over a small rose in a vase. He slid off the bed and placed his feet on the floor.

'I'll take this into my room and study it for a little while.'

She swept past him, making a wide circle round the bed in case he tried to grab her. She wanted to get away. Her heart was pounding now, every time he came near. It disturbed and confused her. She had told herself a hundred times she didn't love him. When she was told to come on the trip, she had talked herself into believing that she was just infatuated. What was the difference between love and infatuation? she mused as she closed the door of her room.

Ten minutes later, Bradly was knocking for her.

She picked up her briefcase and thin raincoat and draped it over her shoulders. Avoiding his glance, she noticed that he was holding an umbrella.

'I listened to the weather forecast.'

'I didn't know you could speak French.' She slid to one side of the taxi as the warmth of his body touched hers.

'Don't be patronizing.' He smiled, issuing the directions to the driver in perfect Parisian French. Secretly pleased, she listened with sheer pleasure at his expertise. To hear him gabbling on to the taxi-driver inexplicably gave her a great deal of joy.

'Your woman is very beautiful,' the taxi-driver said.

'I must be careful, I don't let her get away,' Bradly answered.

Fran kept her gaze averted, fighting the glow that threatened to colour her face. So he thinks I don't understand.

That could be quite amusing. She bit back the grin by clenching her jaws.

Bradly signed a couple of hundred books throughout the morning, before he laid down his pen. 'That's it, I've had enough,' he muttered quietly to her. He looked tired. 'Perhaps we could have some lunch.'

She packed the books into a cupboard on the stand and locked it, then hung a notice saying they would return in a hour. Famished, they both enjoyed the buffet lunch that was laid out in typically French style.

Monsieur Wyatt, a dapper little man looking every inch a publisher, grabbed Bradly's hand. Once again Fran was left out of the conversation, so continued to pick at delicacies whilst still within earshot.

'Your wife?' the Frenchman asked.

'Unfortunately no.'

He turned and before Bradly could say any more, Fran came forward and spouted a volume of conversation in French that took his breath away.

When the Frenchman had departed, Bradly stood watching her. 'Why didn't you tell me you could speak French?'

'You never asked.' She smiled. 'But don't keep referring to me as 'your' woman. I may have been once, but I'm not likely to fall for your tricks again *Monsieur*.'

He looked so fierce, she thought he might hit her, so she grabbed her briefcase and busied herself at the back of the stand when lunch was over.

Fran had time to reflect on what she had said when she was back in her room at the hotel. The day had been a frantic whirl of autograph hunters and old friends who had dropped in to see Bradly, including some vivacious girls who were modelling at the show. She had felt more than a pang of jealousy when he had escorted one of them to the drinks cabinet.

'Fran, I can't seem to find the Cinzano,' he had called across to her.

Swallowing her feelings she had

answered evenly, 'I'm afraid we used it up on your other guests.'

He shot her a look knowing full well she meant other women who had called on him at the stand. 'Get some more, there's a good girl,' he said in a casual but condescending tone.

She left them together, the model doe-eyed and hanging on to his every word. Fran had pushed her way through the crowd to the Press and Publicity office. Within minutes, she was walking back to the stand with the Cinzano, just in time to see Bradly bending to kiss the hand of the beautiful brunette.

Fran could still feel the hurt as she remembered the scene. To see Bradly so close to another woman. Now, in the quiet of her room, she stared down at the signed photograph of him and all the old feelings flooded back. She had tried to hate him, tried to get him out of her mind, but fate had thrown them together again, and she knew he had rekindled the flame of love within her. She wept. As waves of sadness enveloped her, one thing became crystal-clear. She would never love anyone the way she loved Bradly now.

9

Two days later, they had flown from Paris to Venice. The car had stopped on the outskirts of the city and from there the Motoscafo had taken them to their hotel.

Fran had marvelled at the magnificence of the buildings rising from the canals. It was as though they had been thrown back four centuries, and yet the city had an unfathomable vitality about it. The Metropole Hotel was a work of art in its own right and stood opposite St George's Island.

'The Venetians bury their dead on the island,' Bradly said later as they stood together on the balcony watching a large red sun set behind the turrets on the island.

'It's all very beautiful here,' she whispered.

'Of all the places in the world,

Venice is where I most like to be after New York.'

'What about London?' she said, thinking that she'd like Bradly to see her little house.

'I love London in the autumn or spring, crisp and dry, but you can keep your summers.' They both laughed and she shivered slightly.

He took his jacket off and gently placed it around her shoulders. The musky smell on the jacket reminded her again of New York when they had clung to one another by the East River. She felt his arm rest lightly on her shoulders, and knew that he was going to kiss her. The waiting seemed endless and when he made no attempt to come closer she suddenly felt as though he were just teasing again.

'I thought we'd have dinner at nine if you'd like to have a rest for a while.' A slight anxiety had crept into his voice, she noted. Almost as though he were afraid she might not want dinner.

'Yes, I am tired. I'll sort out some

of the itinerary for tomorrow. See you about nine then.'

Her voice sounded cheerful but her heart felt like a lead weight. He had that capacity to charm her into feeling wanted. Why should a person like him, wealthy, handsome and influential, even consider me? she sighed. Their world was poles apart: him in New York, her in London. It was only the fact that our paths crossed accidentally that he even noticed me, she thought as she blew the suds in the bath into a heap and tried piling them up to form peaks. Drying herself vigorously she smothered herself with a perfumed astringent.

I'll have to look for a job somewhere else when I get back to London, she thought to herself: he could do this again and again — every time he has to tour, in fact.

She stopped combing her hair and looked in the glass, and wondered why Grace had landed her in this situation. Grace knew she loved him.

Why didn't she protect Fran from him? She had to admit this puzzled her. The thought crossed her mind that confiding in Grace hadn't done her a lot of good. The idea of leaving the magazine didn't appeal to her. She had met so many writers and authors and learned such a lot. She'd miss Grace, but the knowledge that Bradly could drop in any time made her determined to go ahead with her resignation. With a start, she heard Bradly knocking on the door.

'Just a minute.' She wrapped her robe closer and let him in.

He held an enormous bunch of red roses in his hands. Wide-eyed, she had no alternative but to take them as he thrust them at her.

'For all your hard work so far.'

Fran buried her head in their fragrance. 'They're beautiful.'

He walked past her without asking to be invited in and closed the door behind her. 'What are you wearing tonight?'

'Nothing special. Why?'

'I like that peachy dress, it goes with your hair.'

'A compliment,' she said provocatively.

'If you like. We're meeting some friends of mine. I'd like you to wear it.'

Inwardly pleased, she kept her face bland. She held open the door. 'If you like to wait . . . '

For a second she thought he wasn't going to get up, but he rose and brushed past her, leaving a faint aroma of cologne in his wake. The flowers looked as though they might have been smiling at her, as she touched them, their tight red buds just opening their petals like little laughing mouths.

Later, as they stood on his balcony, watching the moon glisten on the water, he turned her towards him and kissed her, very tenderly and gently, on the mouth. She offered no resistance. That he would try to do this, was inevitable, and it came as no surprise. Bradly noted her pliability in his arms and strengthened his kiss. She returned it with a passion that swept them both along on a tide of longing.

'Fran, my beautiful Fran.' He swept her hair past her ears and held the nape of her neck in his slender fingers.

She let her head fall back. The wine had left her slightly tipsy, and in a state of eager elation. Her lips parted and she reached up to pull his head down towards her lips again and again.

She felt his hand sweep over her breast with such tenderness she might have imagined it. His muscular legs pinned her to the balcony and she felt a dread run through her that if he tried, he could have all of her. Leadenly she felt him whisper to her as he lifted her into his arms. She was vaguely aware of the stillness in the darkened room. He laid her gently on to the bed, and swiftly undressed her.

'No.' She tried to raise her head.

'Don't worry, my lovely.' He held her nakedness to him as he stroked the length of her back and her thighs.

She felt his hands linger and groaned as she clutched his hair. The world stood still, and a great warmth surrounded her.

★ ★ ★

Blinking in the dazzling sunlight, she turned away as Bradly's voice echoed softly in the room.

'I've brought you some orange juice.'

She squinted up at him. 'How did you get in?'

'I had the key.' He held it aloft.

Fran lifted herself on to one elbow, and almost simultaneously felt her nakedness.

He looked down at her. 'I had to put you to bed last night, you were a trifle unsteady.'

Two pink spots glowed on her cheeks, as she tried to remember. 'Did you stay in here with me?' Her voice was tinny and tentative. 'Bradly!' she shouted, watching him stride about the room.

'See you later,' he said, breezing out of the room.

Fran drank the chilled sharp orange juice and hurled the glass after him.

Later, when she had calmed down and composed herself, she packed her case and even laughed when he entered the room and made some quip about the maid thinking they were married. She didn't know why, but she felt happy. Perhaps it was the reality of the situation. At least she was near him, even if he did treat women casually. Any man in his position would, she told herself. So why not enjoy the moment for what it was? When the trip was over he'd fly to New York. She'd stay in London. Fran found the thought too depressing so pushed it out of her mind.

For a minute she stood on the balcony looking across the canal as a black-covered gondola painted with gold slowly made its way across to the Island opposite. Flowers decked the tip and sides and following closely were a few relatives dress in black. The procession was slow and dignified and for some reason she felt she wanted to make a gesture. She broke off a rose and threw it into the canal.

Bradly was silently watching by the door. 'Why did you do that?' he said softly.

'I don't know.' She shrugged. 'This place has me in a trance half the time.'

A haze hung over the canal as the Motoscafo set them down outside the main station. The scene resembled an early watercolour: weak sun shining on a pale grey misty building. Outside the boundaries of the city once more, they sped to the airport. Venice had been on the one hand hectic, on the other serene. The book fair had been better than the one in Paris, and now she was certainly feeling drained.

Six towns and four weeks later they were having a meal in a little town called Meschers sur Gironde near the sea.

'The mussels are good.'

'Delicious.'

There was a comfortable silence between them. The sun was still bright even though it was seven o' clock. The sky an azure blue.

'I'm thinking I could stay here,' she said, throwing back her head and letting the sun warm her face.

'It's raining in London. We leave tomorrow.' That lead weight inside her jolted again. Bradly had been attentive and polite whilst she had organized the tour. She stared out over the sea. It would all end tomorrow, and she would then have to make plans to leave the magazine. Grace would be pleased she had written a lot of articles on the tour, and she had no regrets about how she had been more or less blackmailed into coming. The fact that her heart thumped every time Bradly came near her would have to be lived with. Maybe he had always been out of her league, and she had only just realized it.

Was he bored with her after six weeks? He didn't show it. But then, she reflected, he never showed his true feelings. This was pointless, she thought, mulling over Bradly's motives and past actions.

'Do you fancy going dancing, as it's our last night?'

Danger, she told herself. 'I think I ought to pack,' she lied.

'Oh come on, Fran,' he cajolled. 'The flight isn't until noon.' Trapped. She wasn't sure how he did it but he always had the last word.

By eleven the music had slowed and he was holding her so that she could feel his heart beat with hers. It was dreamlike; they hardly breathed. She closed her eyes and clung to him, never wanting to let him go.

'Shall I take you home?' his voice whispered from afar. He felt her head shaking, and led her off the dance floor, scattered with lovers. Outside in the balmy warm air, he took her to a spot in the grounds of the hotel and in the shadow of the date palm kissed her with an ardour that left her breathless. There were no questions in her mind now. Only the moment. Tonight Bradly was here. Tomorrow he would go away, and she would never see him again. Fran gave herself to him completely, letting him slip the straps from her dress and kiss her waiting breasts.

Later in her room, she let him undress her, with a consciousness that had evaded her in Venice. She wanted him to caress her and love her. 'I want you,' she urged him.

He kissed her hard on the mouth and then, to her consternation, started to get dressed. In the gloom she tried to touch him. He held on to her fingers for one brief moment, touched them with his lips then abruptly left the room.

She lay staring at the ceiling, not knowing why he hadn't wanted her. He had made a fool of her for a second time. Perhaps this was a punishment for walking out on him. No tears would come: only a pain inside that prevented sleep.

The next morning, there was no orange juice. The maid knocked on the door and brought in a breakfast tray.

'Did I order that?' she asked sleepily.

'No madamoiselle, Mr Wyatt asked me to give it to you.'

Fran shut her eyes. So he didn't even want to face her this morning.

When they did meet, he was cheerful and businesslike. 'What was breakfast like?'

'I don't know, I didn't eat it.'

'That was silly, wasn't it? We don't fly till noon.'

'I'm not hungry,' she snapped.

He ignored the dark rings under her eyes and pushed her hair back behind her ears. The movement caused her to toss her head away from him. She just wasn't going to let him play games with her. Not content with teaching her a lesson, he was making sure that she was well and truly hurt.

His good spirits didn't abate through the journey home. Fran slept as much as she could to avoid talking to him, but this didn't seem to upset him in the least. A car waited for them at Heathrow and he drove first to Grace's house and discharged his luggage on to the pavement. Bewildered, she couldn't believe that he would callously send her home, so she made an effort to get out of the car. Bradly, however, closed the door, after winding down the window. He leaned in and looked at her hard.

'I'm flying to New York tomorrow, so I don't suppose I'll see you before then. The flight is at eight.'

'Crack of dawn breakfast.' She tried desperately to keep her voice light. The world was stopping for her and he wasn't even concerned. Now the inevitable was happening, and he was leaving her life for ever, she was savouring these last few moments.

Was this how wives felt, when men went off to war? she wondered. Except that Bradly would not come back. At least the war wives had a fifty-fifty chance of seeing their men again.

'Thanks for all your help, it's been great.' He bent forward and kissed her lips, before she could move. Then swiftly, he pulled away, picked up the cases and walked toward Grace's house.

In a daze, she let herself into the house, and slumped down in the lounge dressed in her raincoat. The shock of their goodbye had numbed her and when she did eventually rise from the chair, it was dark outside.

Dragging herself to the kitchen, she made some tea, but even before half of it was drunk, she cast it aside. She felt listless and thoroughly miserable. She couldn't even see Grace because he was there.

A chill swept through her as she shivered. The house felt cold. She bathed and then sat curled up with a cheese sandwich in front of the television. The phone stayed silent, and she willed it to ring. Tomorrow she'd have to face Grace in the office, and show her the work she'd done abroad. Wearily she slid into bed, worn out with thinking and feeling utterly alone.

Grace breezed in the office, her normal cheerful self. She glanced momentarily at Fran's white face then hugged her.

'How was Europe?' She flung her shoulder-bag over the chair.

Fran summoned all her poise and took a deep breath. It wouldn't be fair to bore Grace with yet more stories about Bradly. 'Wonderful. I loved Venice particularly.'

'The romantic city,' Grace said openly.

'Very.' Fran had been taken off her guard. The word 'romantic' had conjured up memories of their last evening on the balcony when the red sky had played on the water.

'Do you think the tour was a success?'

'Definitely. Bradly must have signed hundreds of pounds worth of books.

They couldn't get enough of him.'

Grace was watching her animated face as she spoke of Bradly.

'Sorry I couldn't tell you who the author was, he thought you'd back out.'

There was a small silence between them. 'I must be honest Grace, I wasn't thinking kind thoughts about you when I found out. But I wouldn't have missed it for the world.'

'You'll be pleased to know that the magazine surpassed its figures and we're now well and truly in the black. We're still getting letters about your Woody Allen article.'

Fran took the computer sheets that Grace was handing her. 'Marvellous. Bradly will be pleased.' The words were out before she could stop herself.

'Bradly is indeed pleased and has asked me to send you back to Venice for the annual fashion show. All the top Italian designers.' Grace smiled. 'You obviously impressed him.'

'Grace, I couldn't go through it a

second time. Will he be there?'

'Fran, this is work. The January issue will have pictures and your coverage.'

'When do I leave?'

Grace handed her a package. 'You arrive Friday.'

Fran flicked through the tickets. 'Metropole again.'

'Most of the designers will stay in the Metropole; you might just get one or two good stories in the bar.'

The misery of Bradly's coolness towards her vanished as Friday came nearer. She had been given a generous allowance to buy clothes.

'You are to buy a peach silk suit. It looks good with your hair,' Grace said as she handed her a cheque. 'The rest is up to you.'

Fran frowned. 'OK, I will, and I've got some clothes that colour in my wardrobe so I'll take those as well.'

'Good. Look smart, Fran. Everyone gets noticed, even the journalists.'

The flight to Venice held a certain magic again for her. The car stopped outside the city as before and the deserted Motoscafo carried its lonely passenger through the late afternoon towards the journey's end.

She felt a nervousness as she neared the Metropole. The whole place was bustling with beautifully groomed models, handsome men lounging around in well tailored suits and eccentric-looking people who stood around the foyer in groups making dramatic gestures and talking in loud voices.

Her room was almost next to the one she had before except that it had been decorated in a soft cream silk bedspread, and matching drapes that festooned the bed, and windows. She gasped at the sheer magnificence of it. The room must have cost a fortune! The porter closed the door and she carefully unpacked and hung up her new clothes.

The phone rang, interrupting her thoughts. 'Dinner will be served in the Florentine room at 8.30, madam. Would madam care to dress for dinner?'

Then there was a click.

Fran felt her stomach turn over. The dining-room would be her first test. She drew back the wardrobe doors and picked out the peach silk which Grace had suggested she buy.

Even before she reached the lower floor, she could hear the excited talk coming from the dining-room. There was a bustle of waiters wheeling in trolleys of food, and the head waiter was inspecting everything. Her nerve nearly left her. She felt so alone, and she'd have to sit there surrounded by all the most stunning models in the business.

'Madam will follow me.' The head waiter was leading her towards the conservatory.

Her table had peach napkins on a peach-coloured cloth. It matched her dress, and so did the roses on the table. She sat down, wondering why everything was so pretty and why everything matched. The waiter poured some wine.

'Is this my table?' She glanced round. 'The table is set for two.'

'That's right.' A deep voice behind her made her spin round.

'Bradly.' She paled at the sight of him. 'Why are . . . you here?'

She had no fight in her now, only resignation as she looked up at him. He pushed his hands gently through her hair and held the nape of her neck.

'There never was any doubt that I'd eventually make you my wife. Nor was there any doubt that I loved you.' His hand tightened as she tried to look away.

'You lied to me,' she said in a small voice.

'No, I didn't lie Fran, but I went to great lengths to stop you from discovering who I was. I needed you to want me for what I was. Not a publishing tycoon.'

'Then you didn't trust me.' She regained some of her spirit.

'How could I? How could you possibly know what marriage has done to me, or women, for that matter?' He loosened his grip and sat down opposite her. He held his palm on the table until she slowly moved her hand on to his. Their eyes never left each other's face. 'I want you Fran. I've never wanted a woman so much in years. I wanted to be sure you wanted me.'

'The flat in Greenwich?'

He laughed, a rich resonance that filled the conservatory. 'A writer friend of mine lent it to me. He has a house in Long Island.'

'He must be a bestseller.' She felt her mood suddenly lightening.

'He is, but he writes in that flat with nobody to interrupt him. What did you think when you saw it?'

She started giggling, then lifted her head through laughing eyes. 'I wanted to throw all the old furniture out, and decorate it.'

'You actually thought I lived like that?'

'It didn't add up,' she admitted. 'The place just didn't have any atmosphere.'

'We had some long talks there.' His eyes bored through her. She tried to remove her hand but he got up, still holding her and pulled her to her feet. 'Tell me with a kiss how you feel about me,' he urged.

She found it impossible to look away, as she raised her mouth to his. The urgency she had felt when they first met returned as soon as his lips touched hers. It was electric. The spell was complete, and they could be one at last.

'There are problems; your wife,' she whispered.

'I got divorced, two weeks ago.' His chin felt slightly rough as he held on to her. 'I'm free for you.'

An ecstatic feeling of joy ran through her at his words.

'Shall we go?' He pulled her towards some steps that led to the water. 'Trust me,' he pleaded as she looked at the blackness. The water lapped almost on to her feet as a gondola glided into view, lit by a lantern, playing soft music, as he helped her down into it.

They lay together in the cushions, his arm tightly round hers. 'Is there room for both of us?' she asked as they drifted under the final bridge back to the Metropole.

'Try and keep me out.' Those were the last words she heard him speak as he bent to retrieve his prize.

THE END

We do hope that you have enjoyed reading this large print book.

Did you know that all of our titles are available for purchase?

We publish a wide range of high quality large print books including:
Romances, Mysteries, Classics, General Fiction, Non Fiction and Westerns.

Special interest titles available in large print are:
The Little Oxford Dictionary Music Book, Song Book Hymn Book, Service Book

Also available from us courtesy of Oxford University Press:
Young Readers' Dictionary (large print edition) Young Readers' Thesaurus (large print edition)

For further information or a free brochure, please contact us at:
Ulverscroft Large Print Books Ltd., The Green, Bradgate Road, Anstey, Leicester, LE7 7FU, England.
Tel: (00 44) **0116 236 4325**
Fax: (00 44) **0116 234 0205**

Other titles in the
Linford Romance Library:

TO LOVE IN VAIN

Shirley Allen

When her father dies in a duel, Anna has no money to pay off his debts and is thrown into Newgate Gaol. However, she is freed by her cousin Julien, who takes her to her grandparents in France. Finding herself surrounded by people she cannot trust, Anna turns more and more to the handsome, caring Patrick St. Clair. Then, to her horror, she discovers her guardians are planning her marriage to a man of their choosing!